CLAIM ME HARD

BRIDGEWATER COUNTY - BOOK 2

VANESSA VALE

Cover design: Bridger Media

Cover graphic: Period Images

GET A FREE BOOK!

PROLOGUE

*H*ANNAH

Their hands were on me. Yes, *their.* Two sets of large, rugged palms skidded over my bare skin, awakening every nerve ending in their paths. I could feel them, one on each side of me. I was sandwiched between two hard, well-muscled bodies, their erect cocks pressing against my hips. They wanted me, that was obvious.

But two men? I was a doctor. My social life consisted of an hour-long dinner break at midnight between trauma cases. The only variation in my wardrobe was whether I would wear green or blue scrubs with my white doctor's coat. My makeup had expired in the second year of med school and my hair hadn't been in anything but a ponytail to keep it out of my face for just as long.

I couldn't lure one man in my bed, let alone two. Well, I'd lured one asshole, but it had never been like this. Never been hot and needy, frantic and...naughty. One found the back of my knee, pulled me wide. The other matched actions so I was on my back, my legs spread. With their hands holding me open, I was at their mercy, available for whatever they wanted to do. And that included a finger very gently circling the top of my clit.

"You're soaking wet through your panties," the voice said, dark and rough. He seemed very pleased that I was aroused for him. I *was* wet; I could feel the silk cling to my folds. Rough stubble abraded my neck as I was kissed. Angling my head, I offered him better access.

I felt a tug at my hip, then heard the rip of my dainty underwear. That was my only feminine concession. Fancy undies. That pair was now trashed, just a wisp of discarded fabric, but I didn't care. A guy just ripped my panties off. I was *not* going to complain.

"Ever had two men before?" The words were whispered in my ear. It was the second man, his voice rougher, if that were possible. Goosebumps rose on my flesh at the sound.

I shook my head, bumped his forehead.

"You're going to love it."

A hand brushed over my bare nipple and I gasped. My body was so responsive, the tip hardening immediately. I arched my back, eager for more. That light caress was not enough.

Yes, I was going to love it.

A finger circled my entrance, round and round, but not slipping inside.

"Please," I begged. I knew what I wanted and it was them, it was everything they would give me.

"Patience. Good girls get just what they deserve," the voice said as his finger slipped inside.

"Yes!"

All at once, I was chilled, the gentle and ardent hands were gone. I no longer felt them surrounding me. I was alone. It was dark and instead of feeling desired, I felt dirty. Scared. Exposed.

"Bad girls get just what they deserve."

That voice.

Oh god. I knew that voice.

It hadn't been the voices of the other men. No, it was Brad.

He was mad. Irate. I cringed, curling up into a ball to protect myself.

I smelled the familiar, cloying cologne. "You're mine. You'll never get away from me."

I sat bolt upright in bed, gasped as I struggled against the sheets tangled about my legs, trying to get away.

A dream.

God, it was all a dream.

No hot men. No Brad.

I was in my new apartment over the diner. Alone. Free from Brad, but hardly free.

I was covered in sweat, my t-shirt damp, my breath coming in harsh gasps. My skin quickly chilled, my nipples hardening. My pussy ached, remembering the way I'd been touched in the dream. My hand slid down beneath the covers, beneath my panties. I was wet and needy from the dream. I wanted those fingers getting me off, even with the crazy idea of it being a threesome. Insane. Unreal. But it had been nothing but a dream. A hot, sweaty dream, but Brad ruined it. Not just in my sleep, but in my waking hours, too.

He ruined everything.

I might have fled LA and his cruel fists, but the voice in my dream had been too true.

I would never get away from him.

Hannah

The diner's pale green uniform was hardly fashionable, but it was comfortable...and comforting. I ran my hands over the polyester blend, took a deep breath. It was a far cry from the scrubs I was used to, but the simple dress with its clean white apron was a throwback to another era, just like this town I'd ended up in. Bridgewater. How the hell had I ended up here? Not just here, as in Montana, but here as in hiding out. Putting my real life on hold because of an asshole ex. Running scared.

That question seemed to run on a constant loop in my brain ever since I stopped in this tiny, blink-and-you'd-miss-it town two weeks ago. While it sat in a picture-perfect valley, it wasn't exactly London. It was far from a vacation destination, and waitressing at a local diner was the polar opposite from the dream career I'd left behind. No one just walked away from ten years of schooling, residency and internships. No one except me. But a woman on the run couldn't be picky, and Bridgewater was as far off the grid as any town could be. And that was the point, wasn't it? I wasn't here on vacation. I wasn't seeing the sights. I was here to hide, pure and simple.

A now-familiar anger welled up and I took a deep breath to get my emotions under control. I glanced at myself in the bathroom mirror. Only a hint of makeup—something had to hide the bags under my eyes—and hair pulled back in a sleek ponytail. Residency didn't offer any time to primp so I was used to going natural. I was also used to the sleep deprived look. But I wasn't pushing a forty-eight-hour shift in the ER. I looked like shit now because I was afraid. And that made me so damn mad! He'd reduced me to this. Half scared, half mad. Honestly, these days I wasn't sure who I was angrier with—my ex for hurting me or myself for running away like a coward. Or for even being interested in the asshole to begin with.

Brad Madison had been the ideal boyfriend... at first. Handsome, attentive, even sweet. But I guessed that was the way it always started. No one got together with a guy she knew to be a monster. They were always sweet and charming, loving and doting. Brad didn't change overnight, either. His downward spiral was slow and insidious. He'd gradually grown more controlling, and over time his words had turned cruel. After several weeks away, it all seemed so obvious. The way he'd manipulated me and made me doubt myself—textbook emotional abuse. I'd seen it all the time in the ER, women who "ran into a door" or "tripped." But that was the beauty of hindsight, it was always twenty-twenty.

I hadn't seen it at the time, even with all the time I spent at the hospital working. The change—in Brad and in our relationship—had occurred so gradually that I'd lost all perspective.

Until he hit me.

Only once, but that was part of the problem. My initial reaction after the shock and fear wore off was to tell myself that it had been only once. I found myself wanting to believe him, that it was a one-time deal. That he really did feel sorry and that he actually would change. That his suddenly kind demeanor was the real him. Worst of all, I found myself falling into a classic trap. I started to blame myself. I'd burnt the eggs. The moment I realized I was making excuses for him was in the ER. I had on plenty of foundation and concealer to hide the bruise on my cheek when a woman came in who'd been beaten up by her husband. I'd begun to tell her the standard lines about the signs, getting out, how there was help available, if she wanted to press charges. Then she looked at me, pointed to my cheek and asked me what had happened. I'd opened my mouth to tell her a lie, then realized, like a light bulb going off, that I was *her*.

I told her the truth, that I'd been hit by my boyfriend —over eggs!

Vowing to her, I said I'd end it with Brad if she walked away from her cruel husband. I'd left the ER that night to make a clean break from him. Or tried to, at least. It took all of my courage to tell Brad it was over, afraid he'd hit me again as I did so. If he'd hit me over burnt breakfast, what would he do when I said I was leaving him? By that point, I was well and truly scared of the man I'd thought was the love of my life.

I had no idea what happened to the patient in the ER. I had to hope she'd gotten help, gotten away. Me? I'd gotten away, but there was no help. Only hiding.

Looking around my bare bones one-bedroom apartment above the diner, I tried to feel appreciative rather than resentful that I'd been forced out of my old life and career. And I *was* grateful. The space was spartan, but clean. The rent was cheap and the commute to work was only a flight of stairs. I'd been lucky to find this place, with its friendly residents. Bridgewater was picture perfect, a western Norman Rockwell town. The fact that there had been a job opening at the old western-themed diner on Main Street had been a stroke of luck. I needed money, money that didn't come from an ATM or credit card that were traceable. I sure as hell hadn't had time to set up a new life for myself before I ran, so I felt lucky.

I picked up my lip balm, swiped it over my dry lips, my thoughts returning to Brad.

After I'd told him I was leaving him, I walked out of his apartment naively thinking that I would never see him again. I'd been relieved. Liberated. What an idiot. Of course, he wouldn't let me go that easily. A few hours later he showed up at my place. I knew he'd been drinking from the glazed look in his eyes, the scent of whiskey on his breath.

You're mine and I'm never letting you go.

Those words still echoed in my skull at night when I should be sleeping. Like the weird dream the night before. A mixture of a hot sex dream and my worst nightmare. The possessiveness of his tone that night, and the sneer—it still gave me chills. The situation had spiraled from bad to terrifying after that. He'd showed up at the hospital when I was on shift, drunk and angry, shouting about how he was watching me. How he'd never let another man have me. Who knows what would have happened if security hadn't arrived?

And then there had been the flowers on the doorstep with a note of apology, followed by threatening messages on my voicemail. His behavior had turned erratic and I knew it was just a matter of time before he crossed the line again from emotional abuse to physical. I'd been trained to talk to women about this, seen firsthand what an abusive guy could do when pushed.

I'd tried to talk to the police, but since nothing had actually *happened,* their hands were tied.

I knew then that if I stayed in LA, the next time wouldn't end in more than a bruised cheek. And so I'd fled.

I turned to face the full-length mirror on the back of the bathroom door. Saw myself now. The uniform, the apron. Goodbye Hannah Winters, hello Hannah Lauren.

Brad was a thousand miles away and so was any danger. Or so I hoped. After two weeks, I was beginning to breathe easier, beginning to sleep longer than a few hours at a time, waking from every little creak of the old building. Or a weird-ass nightmare. I had nothing to fear here in Bridgewater—Brad wasn't here—and that alone was a reason to give thanks. I'd left Los Angeles and he had no way to find me, I'd made sure of that. I may have missed seeing the man for what he was, but I wasn't stupid. I was a doctor. I'd spoken with someone from a shelter about "how to get away" and covered my tracks. Dropped my last name.

The moment he'd left that last night and I was certain he wasn't waiting outside my apartment building, I made a run for it. I'd thrown some clothes in a bag, took cash out of three different ATMs and headed to the bus station. I hopped on the first bus I could find, and then in Salt Lake City, another. Bridgewater just happened to be one of the towns the bus stopped in to give its passengers a short break and a meal. When I stepped off and saw the almost surreal frozen-in-time tableau that was Main Street—well, I figured this little town was as good as any to stop for a while. To hide. I'd stay just until I figured out my next steps.

The bus had left without me and I found myself strolling up and down the six blocks that made up downtown Bridgewater. Main Street was lined with two-story brick buildings that were straight out of the nineteenth century, with stores that sold honest-to-God cowboy hats and boots, along with fishing rods, rifles, and any other outdoorsy equipment one might ever possibly need. It was charming, sure, but not exactly an epicenter of job possibilities. It truly had been a stroke of luck that the diner had a "help wanted" sign posted in the window. Even luckier that the diner's owner, Jessie, seemed to take a liking to me despite the fact that I was an outsider with zero waitressing experience. I'd just gotten off the bus and she offered me a job in the restaurant and the little apartment above it.

So far things had panned out pretty well in Bridgewater. The shifts at the restaurant kept me busy, the locals were incredibly friendly and I was safe from Brad. I was completely under his radar. I forced a smile at my reflection. See? Grateful.

Wide-set green eyes stared back at me from the reflection. At least they were no longer filled with fear— that was something I'd never take for granted ever again. The dark shadows beneath my eyes were gone, too. While I hadn't slept through the night yet, a doctor was used to lack of sleep. Being a small-town waitress hadn't been on my five-year plan when I graduated from med school, but I'd come to find that I liked it, amazingly enough.

The job was hard in its own way, but I relished the distraction. Besides, the manual work might have been difficult, but it was far less stressful than working in the ER. Those I helped weren't sick or dying. They just wanted a cup of coffee or today's special. I missed my job, of course, but taking a break from that kind of life-or-death stress had been a relief. I'd been dealing with enough stress in my life thanks to Brad.

Waitressing was tiring work. For the first time in what felt like ages I was falling asleep at the end of the day and lately woke less and less from nightmares.

Besides, I wasn't going to be a waitress forever. I'd be back to my old job soon enough. My stay in Bridgewater was short-term, just until Brad got deployed. Being in the army, and even as a Lieutenant Colonel, he had to do what he was told and he couldn't tell his commanding officers he wasn't going to be sent overseas. He couldn't hit them if he wasn't happy with them.

He'd mentioned he was being sent to South Korea, to lead a battalion that maintained all the helicopters on the base. He'd be deployed for four years and there was no way he could hurt me once he was gone. I didn't know the exact date he shipped out, but it couldn't be much more than a few months at most until the Pacific Ocean separated us. All I had to do was lay low until he was gone and then I could reclaim the life he'd stolen from me. He'd be in Asia. While I didn't wish what he'd done to me on someone else, I knew he'd probably find some new woman to control and manipulate. Then, he'd forget about me.

I smoothed back my hair, the ponytail not doing much to tame the wild curls. My shift was starting in a matter of minutes and I didn't want to be late, especially because of my stupid daily mental pep talk. The town's diner was always packed at mealtimes and my days flew by as I hustled to keep my customers satisfied.

Two customers in particular came to mind—Declan and Cole. I grinned at my reflection. Now they were customers I would happily satisfy. My soft giggle sounded jarring in the quiet apartment. I hadn't heard my own laughter in far too long. The men in question had come in for lunch during every one of my shifts for the past week and I said a little prayer that today would be no different. To say their presence was the highlight of my day made me sound pathetic. But when I watched them come in the front door and settle themselves in a booth in my section—always my section—I felt like a sixteen year old with a crush on the high school quarterback.

Was it wrong to harbor a crush—okay, two crushes—while on the run? Probably. I may have only packed one small suitcase, but I had plenty of baggage. Seeing those two sexy cowboys made my heart practically beat out of my chest and my palms dampen. Just the sight of the virile duo made my nipples tighten and I was sure that was evident through the thin fabric of my uniform and bra beneath.

They were cowboys, through and through and Jessie had caught me staring. She'd come up to me the first day, leaned in and said they were both tall drinks of water. I'd had no idea what that expression meant, but if it was that they made women's panties wet with just a penetrating stare, then she was exactly right.

Their cowboy hotness worked on me. The broad shoulders, the rugged jawlines, the penetrating stares. Yeah, it totally worked. Every damn day. By the time I crawled into bed at night, I was ready to touch myself as I thought of Declan's blue eyes and Cole's wide smile.

They were gentlemen—Jessie would have warned me otherwise—but their flirtatious comments and flattering attention had me thinking they might be otherwise in private.

Of course it didn't mean anything. Two men flirting with me wasn't serious. I mean, two men? It was harmless fun and I had to admit, it felt good to have them looking at me in that way. Even if it was just for simple flirtation. I felt feminine, even in my less-than-stylish uniform.

It wasn't like I was looking for another relationship and I was certain that they were just intrigued by the new woman in town. Knowing it wasn't serious was what gave me the freedom to flirt right back. I also flirted with Mr. Kirby, who was there every morning at seven for his coffee and toast, but he was eighty-four.

It had been a long time since I'd been so flattered and charmed by any man, let alone two. Especially two. Two hot, sexy cowboys. Living in LA, I'd had no idea a cowboy could melt my butter. But t*wo*! With dark hair and chocolate colored eyes, Cole had that sexy brooding thing going on. Declan, on the other hand, was the living definition of the all-American hero with short, clean cut red hair and blue eyes. He was a cop, that much I knew from Jessie's gossip and the sight of the SUV parked out front with the light bar on top, but I had no idea what Cole did for a living. Looking at his rugged hands, broad shoulders and corded muscles, I had to assume something physical. Something outdoors. A real dang cowboy.

I was certain Jessie knew everything about those men and would happily give me the scoop if I were to ask. That was the beauty of small towns. Everyone knew everything about everybody and gossip was considered a legitimate pastime right alongside knitting and woodworking.

But asking would mean opening up to a stranger—if I asked questions about them, someone might ask questions about me. I couldn't risk it, no matter how curious I might be. I could hide behind playful banter; it kept any probing questions from the hot duo. Besides, I had no interest in telling anyone that I was interested in *both* Declan and Cole. Jessie would just laugh in my face.

In the quieter times between meals, I would let my mind wander as I filled salt and pepper shakers, trying to decide who I liked more. Declan or Cole? A gorgeous ginger or a dark-haired hottie? It had become something of a game to help keep my mind off my problems.

Some days I thought it might be Cole with his smoldering dark eyes and that slightly too-long hair that had a tendency to fall into his eyes. Something told me he would be a touch wild and a whole lot dominant in the bedroom. When I fantasized about him I saw blindfolds and handcuffs. Not typically my sort of thing, but something about Cole made me think I might just like it rough and dirty, as long as he was in charge.

Declan, on the other hand, I fantasized about when I was in the mood for slow, sweet, and seductive. He had an old-fashioned chivalry about him and I was absolutely certain that he knew how to please a woman.

Each of them, I was absolutely positive, would put a woman's pleasure before his own every single time.

There I went again, fantasizing about two men who I'd never see once I moved on from Bridgewater. I wasn't always so obsessed with sex. Never thought about having it with two different men. Clearly, it had been way too long since I'd had an orgasm—much as Brad liked to have control, he couldn't make me come to save his life. He used to, in the beginning, but my pussy seemed to have a better asshole detector than my brain because it stopped buying his lies. For a long time, I'd been telling myself it was me—my sex drive was low or maybe I'd gone frigid. That was a thing, right?

But after a little time away from Brad, I knew the truth. I was horny as hell, just not for his sorry ass.

I studied my reflection one last time, keeping in mind that my two favorite customers would most likely be sitting at one of my tables. Shaking my head, I had to remember playful flirtation was all it was going to be.

Why would they be interested in me? The lip balm didn't make my lips look fuller. The swipe of mascara did nothing to highlight my eyes. And the mint green color of the uniform clashed with my pale skin. I wasn't about to win any beauty contests, but it was fitted enough to show off my small waist and short to show some leg. But I wore my running shoes with it to spare my feet the torture of standing all day. What a look!

I gave one last glance in the mirror, assuring myself that this was as good as it was going to get. Vanity didn't matter since my two crushes were just fantasy material and were going to stay that way. I grabbed my small purse and headed toward the door. My pace quickened at the thought of seeing my two favorite customers again. I was fully aware of how ridiculous it was, of how I was acting. With everything going on in my life, a silly crush and a temporary time out from my stressful job had me feeling almost human again. I couldn't run forever but as I walked into the diner, I couldn't help but think that there were worse things than starting over, even if it was for all the wrong reasons.

2

ECLAN

Cole shifted in the booth across from me and checked his watch for the millionth time. "Maybe she's not working today."

I fought back a sigh. "Jessie said she was working the lunch shift, didn't she? If anyone would know her schedule, it's Jessie. She'll be here, just relax."

Truth was, I was probably just as on edge as Cole, but I was better at hiding it. I wasn't worried that Hannah wouldn't show—the new waitress had never been late for her shift in the past five days we'd been coming to see her—but I still had my reservations. Hannah Lauren was the first woman we'd set our sights on, and the fact that she was a relative stranger who we knew nothing about? Yeah, that definitely put me on edge.

It didn't change the fact that I wanted her—that we wanted her—but my gut told me something was up with her. As a cop, that gut feeling was what had kept me alive before. I listened to it.

In Bridgewater, men knew when they'd found the one. It was custom that a woman shared two husbands, sometimes three. We were raised to listen to our hearts and go after our woman with everything we had. I was born into a family that believed in this, lived this. I had two dads, saw the dynamic between them and my mom. Knew love when I saw it. Knew they took care of her every need. Put her first. Made her the center of their world. I believed in it, and wanted that myself. Cole and I decided years ago we'd share a woman. We just hadn't found her. Until now.

But that voice in the back of my head —the one that made me a hell of a good cop—it was damn hard to silence, even if I did believe that Hannah would be ours.

She was beautiful, there was no doubt about that, and sparks flew whenever she was near. Shit, I got a hard on every time I saw her and I knew it was the same for Cole.

There was no doubt in my mind the attraction was mutual. I didn't need to be a cop to pick up on that. Her bright green eyes seemed to darken when we were talking with her and she blushed whenever we flirted or made a suggestive comment. I'd bet good money that she spent just as much time picturing how we'd be in bed as we did thinking about all the ways we'd fuck her senseless once we made her ours.

So what was the problem? We liked her, she liked us...we should be celebrating the fact that we finally found her, not sitting here staring at each other like two caged animals. Waiting. I knew what Cole's issue was—he had a shit ton of baggage to get over before he could trust a woman after the crap his stepmom put him and his dad through. I'd known that all along and was fine with it. Like my fathers and grandfathers, I knew that once the right woman came along, she'd help Cole get over his past.

I just never thought that I'd be the one with a hang-up when we met her, and my issue was more difficult to figure out. From the moment we spotted Hannah five days ago, I'd known she was it for us. But the more we got to know her—or rather, the more we didn't get to know her despite all our conversations—the more that cop voice told me to slow down and get some answers.

Jessie headed toward our table with a carafe of coffee. She was the only one in this town who knew anything about Hannah who'd appeared out of nowhere two weeks ago. From what I could gather, she didn't know much at all, or wasn't saying. She kept confidences like a damn vault. While I appreciated that, in this instance, I wanted to take her down to the station and interrogate her until she talked.

"She is working today, right, Jessie?" Cole asked.

Who *she* was went without saying. Cole and I hadn't exactly been subtle in our interest.

"She'll be here any minute." Jessie topped off Cole's mug and then mine, a little smile forming on her lips.

She'd run the restaurant with her two husbands longer than I'd been alive. To say that she was pleased we'd found interest in her new waitress was an understatement. She was a blatant matchmaker and we'd avoided her efforts before. But now, now we were seeking her help and she was enjoying watching us squirm.

"Have you learned anything more about where she came from?" I asked. "Or what she's doing here? Is she just passing through or—"

She put a hand on her hip.

"Declan MacDonald, I've told you before and I'll tell you again. I don't know anything more than what I've already told you. If you want to know about the girl, I suggest you ask her yourself."

Cole smirked at me over the rim of his mug. Like a grade schooler, my best friend still thought it was funny to watch me get scolded. I knew he shared my reservations about Hannah, but he seemed to think all the mystery around this woman would be cleared up once we got her out of this diner and into our bed.

"Just curious," I mumbled, trying to avoid Jessie's scowl. Jessie had taken to this new waitress and was as protective of her as if she were her own daughter.

"Every day you ask me the same questions," Jessie said, clucking her tongue as she waited for Cole to hold out his mug to be refilled once more. "If you like the girl, you need to shut off that police brain of yours and get to know her like a regular man."

Her words were truer than she realized. My "police brain," as she called it, was dying to get some answers. Hannah Lauren was a mystery. She didn't even have a car so I couldn't search for her through the DMV. No records popped with her name. Hell, nothing came up when I searched for a Hannah Lauren. It seemed she appeared out of thin air.

My gut was saying there was more to her than she let on, but it was also telling me she wasn't a criminal. Hell, she doted on Mr. Kirby, who was as cantankerous as a cat dunked in the creek. She put up with Sally and Violet, Jessie's friends and town busybodies. Hannah seemed to like everyone. Hell, she even seemed to like us. To a certain point, and there went my gut feeling again.

Jessie's eyes narrowed on me as if she could read my thoughts. "You stop it right now, Declan. She's a sweet girl and I can vouch for her that she's not some serial killer in hiding, if that's what you need to hear."

Cole was outright laughing at my discomfort and I had to fight the urge to punch him in the face as heat crept up my neck. She had a point and I knew it. I'd been a cop since I finished college and that way of thinking was hard to shake. Investigating crimes—even though anything more than teenage pranks or drunk driving were rare in our small town—had made me suspicious. Bridgewater folks tended to trust one another—even strangers. It was a good thing, but sometimes, bad stuff happened to good people.

Jessie had a point and I told her so, which took some of the fuel out of her fire. "All right, then." I'll be damned if Jessie's grin wasn't filled with mischief as she pointed at Cole, then me. "You two should stop wasting time and take the girl out, if you ask me."

Cole and I exchanged a look. We planned on doing just that, given the chance. We'd already agreed that she would be our girl, now it was just a matter of finding a good time to ask her out. We'd wanted to the last few days but she'd been too busy working for us to ask.

"You think so?" Cole never had been one to show his hand.

Jessie nodded. "You bet. Hannah's a sweet thing and pretty as a picture. She'd make a fine wife for you boys."

"I hope you didn't tell her that," I said, trying not to

roll my eyes. While it was great to have Jessie give us some insights into Hannah, a man didn't need a surrogate mother doing his work for him. I was just surprised that my *real* mother hadn't heard of our interest in the new waitress yet. I'd been waiting for the call for days now. "We don't want to scare her off."

Jessie sniffed. "Of course not. I'll let you two tell her that you're a package deal and that you're in the market for a wife. I just told her that you were both fine, available young men." She gave us a wink. "I put in the good word. Now it's up to you two to do the rest."

"We'll do our best," I said. "And I promise, no more cop questions from here on out. I'll get to know her the old-fashioned way."

If the old-fashioned way meant kissing her breathless, learning her curves and what made her gasp, what made her hot, what made her come, then I was all for it.

When Jessie walked away, she wore a satisfied smile at having won her argument.

"You just lied to that nice woman," Cole said as Jessie headed behind the counter. "You're not letting this go, are you? You're like a dog with a bone when you think something's off."

I leaned across the table and lowered my voice. "I'm not going on a witch hunt, if that's what you mean. I just want to know more about her—where she came from, what brought her here. If Hannah really is the one for us, I'd think you'd want the same thing."

Cole pushed the mug back and forth between his hands. He had a harder time admitting that she could be the one and right now I could practically see the gears turning in his brain. "*If* she's the one for us," he said. "We don't know for sure."

I gave a snort of amusement, thankfully just before I took a sip of my coffee. "Now who's the one lying? I've seen the way you watch her. You can't take your eyes off her. Those long legs and gorgeous curves."

He nodded slowly. "I can't deny that. The woman is hot as hell and sexy as sin."

"And..." I prompted. I wanted to hear him say the words.

He frowned. "And you know damn well that I hope she really is our woman."

I tried not to smile—admitting that was tough enough without me laughing at him. I was just glad to know we were in agreement. Hannah was ours.

"There's a connection between the three of us," he said slowly. "And I hope for both our sakes that our instincts are right."

Christ, there was more. "But..."

Cole leaned back in the booth and shook his head. "You know damn well why I have my reservations."

I did, and I also knew that once he got to know

Hannah, he'd get over them. Just like I'd get over mine once she let us in. I had doubts about the woman herself, which could solely be resolved by a few dates. Cole had issues with the past that clouded his judgement where all women were concerned. If Hannah was wife-worthy, then those issues were going to hound him.

"Cole, she's nothing like Courtney. You've got to see that."

Cole's stepmother was a gold digger who'd taken his dad for ride. A cruel and nasty ride. She'd worked her wiles on the grieving widower and married him, only to divorce him a short time later and steal the bulk of his money. With the man's vast property, he'd been Montana wealthy—rich, but didn't flaunt it. Cole, who'd been a teenager at the time, could only watch helplessly as the bitch had crushed the old man's spirit. Cole believed her actions were the reason his father had a heart attack and died a few months later.

It made me bitter, just thinking about what that bitch had done. But Cole? It had made him jaded as fuck, that women weren't to be trusted, especially with his heart. My gut said something was up with Hannah, but it wasn't that she was out for Cole's ranch or his money, which he'd brought back to the way it had been before Courtney, hell, before his mom had died.

He shrugged, but before he could argue the point I stopped him. "She's here."

Cole half turned in his seat to get a look at the woman in question and then we were both shamelessly staring. Fuck, were we whipped. Hannah. She was a breath of fresh air walking through the front door of the diner. Even if I hadn't heard the jingle of the bell attached to the entrance, I still would have known she'd just arrived. Maybe I was a romantic, but I could have sworn the atmosphere shifted and the air grew thick with tension. Need. My damn need. I shifted in my seat as my cock got hard. My brain might have some doubts about her, but my cock didn't.

She spotted us right away and after a brief pause, so brief most people wouldn't have caught it, she kept walking straight back to our booth after dropping off her purse behind the counter. Yes, she came right over to us. She was interested.

God, she was so fucking pretty. I itched to reach out and stroke my finger over her cheek. No makeup and a ponytail and the woman was still gorgeous. High cheekbones and a slight slant to her wide green eyes gave her an exotic look—well, exotic for Bridgewater, at least. Her dark hair was pulled back for work, like usual, and that uniform of hers shouldn't be sexy—hell, there was nothing sexy about it when Jessie wore it—but somehow Hannah pulled it off. It made me want to know what she wore beneath. She was a petite little thing with perky, lush breasts and a sweet, rounded ass. And those legs...shit, I'd been dreaming about having those legs wrapped around my waist from the first moment I saw her.

She came to a stop at our table, her pad and pen already in hand. "Hey guys. I see you have coffee already. What else can I get for you?"

It was the same thing she'd said every day this week. The difference was, this time we'd shown up early and already had our coffee. We didn't need anything but her. The diner wouldn't really start to fill up for the lunch rush for another twenty minutes or so, which meant she could stand and chat. This time, she couldn't run away from us without giving us a chance to ask her out.

Cole wasted no time. "Slow down there, Hannah. You just got to work and no one's here yet. Why don't you have a seat and keep us company for a bit before your shift really starts?"

To back up his words, I slid over in the booth and patted the empty spot beside me.

That right there, in her eyes. I could have sworn I saw wariness flicker across her pretty features before she pasted on that dimpled smile she used with all the customers. She looked around, took in the mostly empty diner. "I don't know if I should—"

"Jessie, tell Hannah a five-minute break is not a crime in these parts," Cole called out.

"I just got here. I can't take a break!"

Jessie's laughter carried across the diner. "Girl, take a load off while you can. You've been running yourself ragged this week with shifts. Donna and I can set up for lunch."

To her credit, Hannah relented with a small smile as she slipped into the booth beside me, although she kept a very blatant few inches between my broad shoulder and her uniform clad small one.

Damn, she smelled even better than I'd remembered. Clean and feminine, the scent of her soap or shampoo, or whatever it was, hit me like a drug. Strawberries, watermelon or something that made me want to lick her all over. "So, Hannah," I said, my voice a little rough with need. "Tell us about yourself."

Cole raised one brow but I ignored him, I was too busy watching Hannah's reaction to the question. That smile never faltered as she shrugged one shoulder. "Not much to tell, I'm afraid. What about you guys? How long have you lived in Bridgewater?"

"Born and raised," Cole said.

"Where did you move here from?" I tried again.

"Oh, I'm from all over." Her smile deepened and I got a flash of that adorable dimple again. "I guess I'm a bit of a nomad."

Cole's gaze met mine and I knew he didn't miss the fact that she'd avoided the question. "Are you from Montana originally?"

He flicked his gaze in my direction and I could read his smirk clear as day. He'd asked that for my benefit. He might think I was being paranoid but he was game to play along, especially when her avoidance tactics were so obvious.

"No, and for that I'm jealous," she said. "I can't imagine a more magnificent place to grow up. You two must have had some great adventures up in those mountains." She pointed out the window in the direction of the Spanish Peaks off in the distance.

Her gaze was guileless when she looked in my direction but I saw the spark of intelligence there—she knew exactly what she was doing and she was doing it well. Hell, she could give a course in misdirection at the police academy.

Sure enough, Cole took the bait and told her a story from our childhood about the time we got caught in a snowstorm while out camping in the woods. It was a story we'd told often enough we could tell it by heart, and Hannah's laugh sounded genuine.

I barely listened, too focused on watching Hannah's reaction and trying to figure out how to ask another question without turning this little chat into an interrogation. By the time Cole's story ended, I realized that maybe he had the right idea. If we wanted her to open up, we needed to share about ourselves first. That was why we wanted to ask her out. Once we took her out on a proper date, hopefully she'd get to know us and then be more willing to open up.

"You won't like it here as much come January when there's three feet of snow on the ground and you haven't felt your toes in two months," Cole said, ending his story.

Hannah started to shift in the booth, getting ready to stand. "I'd better get back to work."

I placed a hand on hers. "Not so fast—"

She jerked her hand out from under mine so quickly it caught me off guard. I kept talking, pretending not to notice the blush that was creeping into her cheeks. But it wasn't shyness or embarrassment that had her pulling away from me. My gut twisted at the flash of fear I saw in her eyes. It was there and gone in an instant, but I couldn't have missed it. Shit, I'd never meant to scare her.

"Don't run off just yet. Cole and I had something we wanted to ask you."

Her shoulders were rigid, but she remained seated. She glanced between the two of us as if she were at a tennis match.

"We'd like to take you out tonight," Cole said.

Her confusion was clear as day as she looked between us. "What, like a friend thing?"

Cole and I exchanged a look before I explained. "Not a friend thing. Definitely not a friend thing."

3

ECLAN

"Oh," she said, that one word as wilted as her shoulders.

"More than a friend thing. Much more," Cole added. "A date with me and Dec."

"Both of you?" she asked, wide eyed.

"See," I began. "Bridgewater is a bit unusual in its ways..."

"Its ways," she repeated slowly as if that would help to clear up my ambiguous statement. Obviously, Jessie hadn't told her.

"Bridgewater was founded by people who believed

that a woman should always have someone around to take care of her...to cherish her," Cole said.

She blinked rapidly like Cole was speaking a foreign language that didn't compute.

I figured it was best to get it over with quickly...rip off the Band-Aid, so to speak. "Here in Bridgewater, oftentimes a woman marries two men."

After a brief silence, Hannah let out a loud laugh. "Two men. Right," she said, dragging out that word. "You're kidding, right?"

As if on cue, the bell above the front door jingled and in walked my sister, Cara, and her two husbands, Mike and Tyler. While I had never been keen on my little sister even dating, I had to admit her men put a ring on her finger once they had her in their sights and were good to her. I nodded toward them. "See for yourself. That's my sister, Cara, and her husbands."

Mike wrapped an arm around Cara's waist as they headed toward a table in the back and Tyler took her hand, entwining their fingers. Hannah couldn't doubt my words; my sister and I shared the same very red hair.

"Oh my God." Hannah said it quietly, under her breath as she openly stared, but Cole and I heard her. She scrambled out of the booth to stand. "I, uh...I've got to get to work."

While more customers were starting to file into the

restaurant, it was hardly slammed. "Stay, Hannah," I said.

Was it my imagination or did she flinch? I knew the Bridgewater way was an adjustment, especially for an outsider like Hannah, but she was jumpy instead of surprised.

"Don't judge until you've seen it in action," Cole said, looking up at her. "The divorce rate in this town is extremely low and the relationships last a lifetime."

Longtime Bridgewater residents—and busybodies— Violet Kane, and her friend, Sally Martin, settled into the booth behind us and didn't pretend to hide their eavesdropping.

"They hit you with the news, huh?" Sally said, her laugh deep and boisterous. The real estate agent had lunch every weekday in the same booth and wouldn't have missed our own daily presence in Hannah's section. She had two husbands and so did Violet, whose son Sam —with his cousin Jack— had just gotten engaged to Katie Andrews. The ladies were very familiar with the Bridgewater way. They lived it, even passed it onto their children. "You should see your face."

Violet held up her ring finger and showed off her wedding band. "Thirty-five years strong with my two men."

"That's, uh... that's great." Hannah's smile had

returned but she was clearly still stunned. "Two men. Wow."

I caught her gaze, bringing her focus back to us. "So what do you say? Will you go out with me and Cole tonight?"

Cole gave her that lopsided grin that all the ladies seemed to love. "Just one drink, darlin'."

Her eyes were wide and after a second of silence she shook her head as if to clear it. "Sorry, just...I can't believe I'm being asked out by two men at once. I admit, I haven't had much luck with just one." She reached a hand up and pushed back an errant lock of hair and I noticed the way her hand shook. "So, how does this work? Do you guys always go on dates together?"

I shook my head. Voices came through my police radio on the table and I adjusted the volume to low. If there was an emergency, a tone would come through first. "Not always. You're special."

"Sp—" A wariness made her smile falter. "Special, how?"

"You're ours." Cole's voice was low and surprisingly possessive. I shot him a warning look when Hannah took a small step back.

"I don't belong to you," she said, her tone sharp and her eyes angry.

I wanted to see that flirty smile on her lips again. Instead, her cheeks were pale and if looks could kill,

Cole would be dead by now. This was not how I wanted this to go. Fuck, we were blowing it.

"What Cole's trying to say is that we're interested in you. As more than friends. We think you might be the one," I said quickly. Then I had to explain how in Bridgewater, men knew instinctively when they'd met their match. How it was fated.

Her brows were drawn together in disbelief but she didn't try to laugh it off. "And that's what you think? That I'm destined to be...what, your wife?"

"We think so, yes," Cole said. His reply lacked the possessive tone from just a moment before, but he was deadly serious and let that show in his eyes.

"But we'd like to take you out so you can see for yourself," I added.

"That you'd make good husbands? Both of you," she said, as if this fact bore repeating. "At the same time."

I caught Cole's smirk, but she didn't seem to notice, thank god. She was busy looking at Sally and Violet's booth to see if they were overhearing. I had no doubt they were.

"That's right," Cole added.

We were supposed to be asking this woman out as gentlemen and I sure as hell didn't want to scare her off with talk of threesomes. Not yet, at least. She was skittish enough as it was. We needed to ease her into the idea, not club her over the head and carry her off to our bed. At least not yet.

But how did you tell a woman you wanted to claim her with another man? How did you tell her we weren't playing games, that were dead serious about it? About her? How did we do that with a woman who seemed to have a very obvious dislike of possessive men? I tried the laid back approach.

But Cole, apparently, had other ideas. He leaned forward and caught her hand. "At the same time and in every way imaginable. You belong between us, Hannah. We'll make you see that."

I knew what would happen, and I was right. She pulled her hand away and stepped back with such haste I thought she might trip. Shit. I shot Cole a warning look. Apparently, he hadn't noticed her reaction when I'd touched her hand. Whatever this woman was hiding about her past, she was scared and we'd only made it worse. It was obvious she'd had boyfriends who were a little too possessive and that didn't sit well with me. Someone with that in her background could easily misconstrue our interest as being a little overpowering. Obsessive even.

I kept my voice low and calm and didn't try to move toward her. "Hannah, we're sorry. We're not trying to push you into anything, I swear, but we've been interested in you since we first laid eyes on you. We've been by every day since hoping to just see you smile our way."

My honesty seemed to help, for her stance relaxed a bit.

"Sally and Violet, hell, even Jessie, can vouch for us." I couldn't see the ladies behind me, but I had to assume they were either nodding their heads or offering thumbs up signs. Cole was looking over my shoulder and grinning.

"We just...like you and want to get to know you better."

That was a total lie. We didn't just like her. We wanted her. Knew she was going to be ours.

Her eyes flicked to the ladies, but she still looked wary. At least she wasn't running away. She stood next to our table at a safe distance and toyed with her pad and pen. Her gaze shifted from me to Cole and back again.

"If I were thirty years younger, honey," Sally called. "I'd give you a run for the money when it comes to these two. You have to admit, you've got two hot men ready to make you theirs. They're not creeps, they're Bridgewater men. That's the way they're made around here. Big, dominant and too sexy for their own good. If they said they wanted me between them, do you think I'd be sitting here? Hell, no. Go for it, and by *it*, I mean them."

I had to remember to send Sally a bunch of flowers later for her help.

To my surprise I caught something more in Hannah's eyes—something hiding behind the fear and the wariness.

Attraction. Yes! It had been there all along like we'd thought. There was chemistry between us. Shared chemistry. But we'd scared her off with our fuck-all fumbling.

"We're pretty bad at asking a woman out, aren't we?" I asked, watching as she nibbled at her bottom lip. "Give two idiots a shot."

"He's the idiot," Cole countered. "I told you I want you, want you between us. I can't fuck that up."

I looked over at Cole, who took a sip of his coffee with an unbearably smug expression. Maybe he wasn't such an idiot after all. If it was fantasies of being with the two of us that got her to give us a chance, I was all for it.

But she hadn't said yes yet and I was afraid to push too hard. She might be tempted, but one nudge the wrong way and she would bolt.

Fate, in the form of nosy neighbors, intervened.

Violet added to Sally's words. "Girl, if you let these boys slip through your fingers, you'll regret it. And if you're worried about all that caveman talk, they mean it in a good way. Trust me. Heck, trust practically every married woman in town."

Hannah turned a pretty shade of pink as it became obvious that the tables around us, which had been filling up with lunch customers, were making this their business. Yes, everyone knew we were interested in her. Hell, we'd been coming here all week. But no one piped up and said it was wrong for her to have two men outright tell her they were interested in making her their wife. Just the opposite. We had the town on our side.

Cole gave her a wink.

"It's true. Everything they've said since we began eavesdropping," Violet added. "I've known these boys their whole lives. You couldn't ask for two finer men. Right, Jessie?"

Jessie was walking past with a tray filled with food. "I've already told her she'd be crazy not to let these boys show her a good time. Lord knows she needs it."

Hannah's blush deepened as she fixed her stare on my hands, on the table...anywhere to keep from making eye contact. Jessie had clearly hit the nail on the head. This woman needed to be shown a good time. And we'd be the men to give it to her. Maybe an orgasm or three would help this woman relax and open up a bit.

Shit. I hated having to admit that Cole was right, but it seemed he'd known what he was doing from the start. Appeal to Hannah's sexual interest and let her see for herself how great the three of us could be. "Go out with us?"

She finally looked up at me.

I dropped my voice and let her see the desire I'd been

trying to hide. "Will you give us the chance to show you a good time?"

She licked her lips and my cock hardened instantly. I could tell she was thinking about *how* we'd show her a good time. Fuck, this woman was turned on and just knowing that she was just the slightest bit curious had me primed and ready to go. I could run with curious and up that to interested and take that a step further to aroused. What I wouldn't give to taste those sweet lips, and other parts of her.

My sister's sudden arrival at our table was the cold shower I needed to stay in control, to remember everyone was watching us. And listening in. And butting in.

"What's going on over here?" she asked with a teasing grin. "Everyone in this place is watching you guys try to land the hot new waitress. With not much success, I might add, based on the look on her face."

Hannah laughed at that, which broke all of the tension in her body, and my sister's smile grew. "Hey, I'm Cara."

"Hannah Lauren." She nodded. "Nice to meet you."

My sister, who was several inches taller than Hannah, threw an arm around her like they'd been best friends forever. "So what's the hold up, lady? You need another woman to vouch for these guys? I can tell you right now you couldn't do any better, even if one of them is my annoying older brother."

Cole let out a snort of amusement and looked up at Hannah. "She has to say that. Dec's a damn pest."

"And you're practically my brother, which makes you just as annoying," Cara added. She turned to Hannah. "It's true. I'm not exactly unbiased." She lowered her voice as if that would keep the eavesdroppers from listening. "But from one woman to another, I can tell you that you'd be missing out if you didn't give the Bridgewater way a try."

She glanced over at her table, where Mike and Tyler were sitting, and Hannah looked, too. My sister's whisper was loud enough for me and Cole and everyone around us to hear. "Seriously, girl. You owe it to yourself and all womankind to give these guys a shot."

With one over-the-top wink she dropped her arm and headed back to her table, calling out, "We need to grab drinks soon, Hannah. I'll give you all the juicy gossip on my brother."

Hannah turned back to me, those bright green eyes still filled with laughter. Sweet Jesus, she was stunning.

"So what do you say?" Sally called out.

Christ, we had the entire town in on this asking out thing. I wasn't sure if Cole and I were totally pathetic or if Hannah needed a little more coaxing than most.

"Thanks everyone, I think Hannah's gotten the point," I said.

All eyes were on Hannah and she gave in with a smile. "Sure, why not? Besides, everyone will hate me if I don't go on at least one date with you. With both of you."

"I heard that," Jessie said, walking past again. "Now that it's settled, let the girl get back to work."

Hannah offered us one last smile before she ran off to take an order at one of the new tables that just sat down. I looked over at Cole, who was leaning back in his seat looking too fucking pleased with himself.

"You know she just agreed to go out with us to get everyone off her back, don't you?" I asked.

That didn't seem to affect him. He shrugged it off. "Whatever it takes to get her between us. Doesn't really matter, does it? If she's the one, we'll prove it to her. We just need a chance."

I couldn't argue with that. If we had the opportunity, we'd show her what it would be like between us. As in in bed together, Cole beneath her, her body pressed into his, and me, behind her, taking her until she cried out her pleasure.

Still, I watched her carefully as we ate our lunch and she ran around the restaurant taking orders and delivering plates full of food. We lingered over our meal; neither of us wanted to walk out of there without confirming our plans.

Cole might talk big, but even he could see that her yes had been coerced out of her by our well-meaning friends. Hell, practically the whole damn town.

Finally, when there was a lull in the lunch business, she ended up back at our table. Sally and Violet had gone, and so had Cara and her men. Wiping her hands on her apron, she gave us a wry smile then bit her lip. "Everyone's gone now, so...um. Look, we don't have to go through with this date—"

"Oh no, you're not backing out on us now," Cole said, holding up his hand.

I kicked him under the table but at least this time Hannah didn't seem too spooked by his possessive tone. In fact, she acted like she hadn't heard him at all. "I'm sure everyone is right, and you're real nice guys. But the fact of the matter is, I'm not looking for a relationship with one man, let alone two."

"You might not be looking, but it found you," I said.

Her laughter was soft and sweet. "I appreciate it, I really do. But I don't think one night is going to change my mind. We can all just save ourselves a little time."

That right there—it sounded like a challenge. I met Cole's gaze and knew he was thinking the same thing. If she gave us one night, we'd make sure she'd be begging for more.

Cole leaned forward, but this time he didn't try to grab her hand. Maybe he was catching on, after all.

"Look, darlin', this won't be a one-night stand. You belong with us—in our bed and in our lives. Give us one night to show you that. If you want out after that, we'll let you go."

Her lips had parted when he mentioned our bed. Holy hell, I was hard as a rock. Her mind might be telling her otherwise, but she wanted it. Us. Her nipples were hard. They were at eye level and that damn uniform did nothing to hide them. Hannah wanted it—us—and I couldn't wait to give it to her. But I wouldn't force her. Waiting for her response was killing me.

Finally, she gave in with a sigh. "All right. One night. But no promises after that."

I grinned at her. "Fair enough. We'll pick you up at seven and take you to the Barking Dog—it's not fancy, but we like it."

She straightened a bit. "You don't have to come to my place. I can meet you there."

Cole was trying to smother a laugh and failing. I smiled up at her. "As a cop, I admire what you're doing. You shouldn't tell strange men where you live. But as a Bridgewater resident, I've got to tell you...it's pointless. Everyone knows that the new waitress lives upstairs. Besides, we're gentlemen and we'll pick you up at your door."

She let out a sigh of resignation. "Okay, fine. I'll see you at seven."

We watched her walk away, that perfect little ass swaying beneath the uniform's skirt. I couldn't wait to get her out of that damned dress and into our bed. Tonight. We had one shot to blow her mind and let her see how good this could be.

Right. No pressure.

4

ANNAH

This was a mistake. I knew it was a bad idea when I'd said yes—when I'd been coaxed by half the town to go out with Cole and Declan—but as soon as I opened the door and found my two very hot dates standing on my doorstep, I couldn't bring myself to care. Maybe it was the fact that I hadn't been the object of so much flattering male attention for years...if ever.

They stood side-by-side on the small landing at the top of the stairs. They both wore button up shirts and jeans, but that was where the similarities ended. Declan was a few inches taller than Cole, but leaner.

Cole's broad shoulders would knock his friend off the landing if he turned a bit. Declan's russet hair was a little damp, as if he'd just gotten out of the shower, and that had my mind veering in the wrong direction. They held their hats in their hands and their eyes, well, their eyes were focused square on me. They liked what they saw and let it show in their heated gazes.

I was in trouble here and I hadn't even said hello.

Was it the fact that I was smack dab in the middle of a man dry spell or was it these men in particular who had this effect on me? When Declan took my elbow and led me down the steps, even opened the door for me and lifted me up into the cab of Cole's truck, the rational part of my brain that had been telling me what a terrible idea this was all afternoon went completely silent.

Instead, my senses seemed to be in charge. And god, were they in heaven. I tried to focus on where they were taking me but I couldn't stop fixating on the feel of their thighs pressed against mine. They were all warmth and strength beneath those faded jeans and it took all of my willpower not to shift so I was pressing against them even harder. Maybe reach a hand out and feel one of those muscular thighs.

What would Declan do if I ran a hand up his leg? Or Cole? He might be driving, but something told me he'd be more than happy to pull over and take me right here and now if given half a chance.

A shiver raced through me.

"Are you cold?" Declan reached out and turned down the AC even as he asked.

"I'm fine." God, get a grip. One would think this was my first-time dating.

Although, to be fair, it was my first time dating in quite a while...and absolutely my first time dating two men at once.

"So, where are we headed?" That was the best my brain could come up with. Holy shit, these guys smelled good. Naturally good, not like one of those metrosexual guys who smelled nice because they were wearing cologne. Or worse, that body spray shit. No, these guys smelled like soap and earth and male.

"The Barking Dog, the local bar," Declan said.

Right. They'd told me that earlier. I was a doctor and these two men were reducing me to a brainless twit. I clasped my hands together in my lap to keep from fidgeting. Maybe Cole noticed, because he reached down and squeezed mine gently before letting them go. His touch was firm, yet gentle. Warm, but I felt rough callouses. It made me shiver all over again.

I was starting to get a little better about not overreacting to their touch. It took me by surprise the first few times they reached for me like they had every right to be in my personal space. But I supposed I was getting used to it, or maybe I was starting to trust them a little. Enough that I didn't think they had any ill intentions, at least, not on the drive across town.

Aside from having Jessie's approval, and the rest of the crowd at the diner, they'd been nothing but gentlemen from the moment I'd met them. Attentive. Curious. Driven.

And tonight, they'd been chivalrous to the point of old-fashioned. At seven on the dot they'd shown up at my doorstep as promised. I was wearing the only nice outfit I'd brought with me—a simple black dress with short sleeves and a short skirt. It wasn't crazy sexy but it fit better than that damned uniform. Between the dress, some makeup, and my hair down around my shoulders rather than up in the requisite ponytail, I actually felt pretty for the first time in a while. And the size difference between us, the way they were so gentle and attentive, they made me feel feminine.

They hadn't tried anything back at the apartment or after they'd helped me into the truck. So maybe it was true. They just wanted to date me. Both of them. If someone had told me a couple weeks ago that I'd be on a date with two sexy studs in Montana, I would have laughed my ass off. It was hard to believe that these two guys really meant it when they said they wanted me to be the one—I mean, who said that? But they seemed to be sincere.

Sincere, yes. But they'd also said some things that made my panties damp. They'd said they didn't want to be friends. They wanted me between them and I knew that didn't just mean in the truck. While they were being gentlemen, I had no doubt if I gave them the green light, they'd be anything but.

They said they wanted me to be their wife. Who said something like that after only a few conversations?

It should freak me out. It did. God, it did because I had a feeling these two were actually serious. But it didn't matter. I didn't have to even worry about even the possibility because I wouldn't be around long enough to get too involved. Once Brad was shipped overseas, then I could return to my life. Go home to LA and get back to being a doctor.

But I could enjoy this one night, at least. I deserved a nice night out with two gentlemen who seemed intent on showing me a good time. And if I wanted more? I could have a wild night in between two hot cowboys. I'd be stupid not to. They were gorgeous and I had a very strong feeling they knew what they were doing in bed. And for one night? I squirmed in the seat, my panties definitely ruined.

Knowing I was the one in control here, not two big, dominant cowboys, allowed me to let go of some of the nerves that had me sitting up, my spine straight as a rod. I let myself rest back against the truck's bench and was rewarded by a smile from Declan that made my mouth go dry.

When we got to the bar, which had a Wild West saloon vibe going on, it became obvious that these guys knew everyone. As we passed a wall lined with booths, it seemed that people at every table were shouting out greetings.

I recognized Cara and her men when they waved to us, but my guys hustled me toward an empty booth, not stopping to introduce me to all their friends. It didn't come across as impolite, more they wanted me all to themselves. Cole slid in first and I sat next to him. To my surprise Declan sat on the other side of me so all three of us were on the same bench—nice and cozy.

Well, maybe cozy wasn't the right word for it. Their thighs brushed against mine again, their arms, too. I could feel the hard muscles on either side of me. It was impossible not to think about what those muscles looked like, what they would feel like beneath my palms. I was trapped between them but I wasn't scared—I liked it. For the first time in a long, long while I felt completely protected from the rest of the world.

Declan hailed down a waitress and they turned to me to order first. Ladies first. God, did they still abide by that rule here in Montana? Maybe I'd found the last place where chivalry wasn't dead.

When the waitress walked away they angled their bodies so they were both facing me. "So, Hannah, why don't you tell us a little about yourself," Declan said. "Where are you from?"

Ugh. Now this was the part I'd been dreading. I'd gotten pretty good at avoiding direct answers but it was hard to relax when I could screw up at any moment and reveal too much. Hadn't they asked me this already? Clearly, they wouldn't let up unless I started giving some answers.

"I grew up on the east coast. So, do you guys come here often? You seem to know everybody."

"Did you move here from the east?" Cole asked.

I met his gaze and looked away quickly. It was too intense. Like he could tell that I was being vague on purpose. I looked to Declan but his expression didn't put me at ease. Oh, he was smiling. He always seemed to be smiling, but I'd bet money that beneath that aw-shucks cowboy exterior, his police officer's brain was working on figuring out the mysterious new waitress.

Shit. Maybe if I shared a little more, they'd ease up a bit. I cleared my throat—after keeping silent for so long, it was surprisingly hard to talk about myself. "No," I said. "I moved to California for college and never left."

There. That was the truth.

"Where'd you go to college?" Declan asked. He

grabbed a peanut from the bowl in the middle of the table and started shelling it.

"Stanford."

All eyes were on me and I knew what their next question would be before they asked it. "What have you been doing in California since graduation?" Declan said.

I gave them my best innocent smile. "Enjoying the sunshine." It was a joke I'd made often at the diner instead of a real answer. This time? It definitely didn't work.

Cole took a sip of the beer the waitress set in front of him. "Were you waitressing?"

Not exactly. For a second I had the urge to confide in these men. Tell them all about how I'd just recently been accepted to join a practice in LA. After all those years of work at my residency and as an intern, I'd finally reached my goal. How nice it would be to tell these guys about it. But I couldn't. I had to stay hidden, head down, until Brad was gone. Any chance of being found would be dangerous for me, and anyone else. If Brad knew I was going on a date with another guy? He'd flip. But two men? I didn't even want to consider it.

Instead, I said, "I was in between jobs. That's part of the reason I left. It seemed like as good a time as any to see the country."

I caught the look they gave each other. Before either of them could start in with more questions, I wanted to get them talking instead. "What about you? What do you do?"

Cole told me about his family's ranch, which he now owned and ran. As a city girl through and through, ranching was something I knew nothing about but he patiently answered my many questions. I had no idea cows were so complicated. Declan told me how he was a cop, which I already knew, and how it was what he'd always wanted to do, ever since he was a kid. Tonight, he wasn't on duty; no radio, no gun on his hip.

"He's serious," Cole added. "This guy used to run around the playground pretending to arrest the bad guys at recess."

I laughed at the image. "So you two go back a long time, huh?"

"We've been friends since kindergarten," Declan said. "Maybe even before that."

Cole nodded. "When I was seventeen my dad passed away and I moved in with Declan and his family until I turned eighteen and took over the ranch." The two men exchanged another look and I got the distinct impression that they were somehow silently communicating.

"That was the year we decided that we would take a wife together."

5

ANNAH

Oh. What the hell was I supposed to say to that?

"I was raised in a Bridgewater family," Declan continued. "Two dads, one amazing mom. They set a great example. After they hear about tonight, I'm sure they'll stop in at the diner to get a good look at you."

Cole gave me a small self-deprecating smile. "I only had one father...and he was miserable. In his marriage to my stepmom, at least. When I went to live with Declan's family..." He trailed off with a shrug, but his point was clear. He'd seen the type of family he wanted to have.

While the whole threesome thing was still a foreign

concept, hearing them talk about it like this—like it was normal and healthy—made it sound almost sweet. Romantic, even.

"Speaking of family," Declan said.

I looked up to see Cara heading in our direction with a friendly grin. "Hey guys. Hannah, good to see you again."

"You, too," I replied. And I meant it. I might not have known her for long, but there was something so comfortable about Declan's sister. She had the kind of open, genuine personality that would put anyone at ease —even me. Her red hair and blue eyes matched her brother's, but she wasn't overly tall like he was. When she stood between her two men, she looked tiny, just as I assumed I looked when surrounded by Declan and Cole.

"What are you and your men up to tonight?" Cole asked.

It sounded so strange talking about Cara having two husbands as if it was normal. Here, it was. I was the odd one around here, not understanding the lifestyle.

"We're meeting up with Katie and the Kanes." She pointed to the bar where a pretty blonde was sandwiched between two attractive men.

I knew the answer before I even asked, but I still turned to Declan for confirmation. "Let me guess, another Bridgewater relationship?"

He nodded. "Katie was friends with Cara back when

we were kids. You met Sam's mom today at the diner. Violet. Katie used to come here every summer to stay with her uncle. When he passed away last year, he left her the property."

Cara cut in. "She came back to sell the place, but then she met Sam and Jack."

Katie headed in our direction and Cara turned to Declan and Cole, crossed her arms over her chest. "You guys need to go get some drinks at the bar."

"We already have our drinks," Cole protested.

His comment was met by a formidable scowl. "Get some more then. We need a little girl time."

Declan and Cole did as they were told but not without a fair amount of good-natured grumbling. As they walked away, Katie joined us and Cara made the introductions. The two women slipped into the booth across from me. "Sorry to run off your dates like that but I had a feeling you might need a minute to process the whole threesome date thing. It takes some getting used to."

Katie nodded. Her dark hair was pulled back in a loose ponytail and I couldn't miss the big diamond on her ring finger. "It's weird at first, I know. I was exactly where you were last summer. Like, in this bar and getting it on with Sam and Jack."

"I remember that night," Cara added, then frowned. "What do you mean getting it on in the bar?"

Katie flushed a bright pink, then grinned. "Let's just say there's a quiet hallway past the bathrooms if you have an, ahem, itch that needs to be scratched."

My mouth fell open and Cara started laughing. "You didn't."

Katie grinned and looked too damn happy for her own good. Glancing at her men, I could see how they might be able to keep her smiling all the time. "We *so* did."

"You'd just met them, at least as an adult, that day!"

"I know. That's why I'm telling Hannah." Katie looked to me. "Bridgewater men are different, if you hadn't noticed. When they say they want you, they mean it. Which means, there's nothing wrong if you want them right back. And those two? Cole and Declan." She bit her lip and eyed them like they were decadent desserts.

"One of them is my brother," Cara groaned. "I don't want to know anything about his sex life." She shuddered. "Do you want them? I mean, *want* them?"

I glanced at Cole and Declan, who were standing at the bar talking with both Katie's and Cara's men. One of them was holding his hands out as if measuring a fish. All six of them were gorgeous. If word got out that Montana men were so hot, the state would be much more crowded.

"Is there something in the water here? I mean, they're all—"

"Hot?" Katie asked, then giggled.

"Yes, hot." I took a sip of my beer. "I'm intrigued by them. Declan and Cole," I clarified.

Oh, who was I kidding? I was way more than intrigued. I was fascinated. Obsessed. I'd been fantasizing about both men since that first time they came into the diner, but it had never occurred to me that I might be able to have both. And holy shit, I could feel myself getting wet at just the thought of being fucked by two men at once. I had a vague idea how it was done, read some steamy romance novels with it, but I could only imagine what it would be like in real life.

If I was imagining how it would be to fuck two men, then it had officially been way too long.

"Intrigued?" Cara asked.

The fact that Declan was her brother and Cole was as good as a brother had me hesitating. Not that I was going to bad-talk the guys, but it was hard to be totally honest.

She seemed to understand my hesitation. "Look, I know I'm biased, but I mean it when I say that if Declan and Cole are showing an interest in you—which they clearly are—then they are serious about this. They've never been like this before."

Katie nodded at her friend's comment. "It's true. These Bridgewater guys aren't like most men. I came from New York where there are a whole bunch of assholes, including my ex-husband. They're not looking for a one-night stand. That whole 'the one' thing they're always going on about? It's the real deal."

"Good to know." It wasn't that I didn't believe them when they talked about finding the one, or even that they hoped I might be that woman. I believed they meant it—and that in and of itself was flattering. But I couldn't believe it would be more than just this one night. I came from a different world, and I'd be heading back to that world just as soon as I was able.

"There are a few characteristics that you'll find are true of the men who adopt the Bridgewater way," Cara said. "They are loyal, sincere, chivalrous...and possessive."

"Oh yeah." Katie nodded emphatically. "That is definitely true. And judging by the way your men are staring at you right now, it's obvious that they've got their sights set on you."

I glanced over at the bar once again and saw that Cole and Declan were, in fact, staring at me and their expressions and posture looked like they might leap over the tables between us and scoop me up at any moment. *You're ours.* That's what Cole had said, and though he might not have meant it to sound frightening, it sounded way too much like the words Brad had spoken that night before I ran. He'd not only been possessive, but he'd been obsessed. Would Declan and Cole be like that? I didn't get that vibe, but I'd been wrong about Brad, too, and look where that got me. Hiding in a town in Montana.

I looked down at my drink as I tried to figure out a nice way of phrasing my next question. "When you say they're possessive...?" I couldn't figure out a way to finish, but both women seemed to know where I was going with that statement.

"Possessive as in protective," Cara clarified, slowly circling her pint glass on the glossy wood table.

"Bridgewater men put their woman first, always," Katie said. "They believe in making sure she is always taken care of—her problems are their problems. It's their duty to make sure she's happy."

"And satisfied," Cara added with a waggle of her eyebrows that had all three of us cracking up. They'd made me feel better and reassured me that Declan and Cole weren't like Brad. What they said only reaffirmed what my gut had told me from the moment I'd met them. They were good men—kind men. They were also sexy men and they were watching me.

"So what's the verdict?" Katie asked, biting her lip to obviously keep from grinning. "Are you interested?"

I opened my mouth to respond and paused. Was I? The ache between my thighs was my answer. But that's not what she meant. I had no doubt she'd be fine with me jumping her brother and his friend for a wild night, but she probably didn't want to hear about it. She was more interested in whether I wanted to become her sister-in-law. "I, uh...I don't know. This is um, well, the first date, so marriage isn't really on my mind. Besides, I hadn't planned on sticking around for long."

"You don't have to know tonight whether you're serious about them," Cara said. "At this point, you just need to know if you're attracted to them. If you are, the rest is up to them."

"Them?"

Katie nodded authoritatively. "Believe me, last summer I was in the same boat you're in right now. I didn't intend to stick around but my men showed me how good it could be if I did."

"I take it they made a good case in the back hallway?" I asked.

She gave me a smug grin. "Oh yeah. And I can happily say that staying in Bridgewater was the best decision I ever made. But what about you? Forget long term, are you interested in these guys?"

Cara and Katie were watching me closely. There was no way I could bring myself to lie. "Yeah," I said. "I'm interested." I glanced back over at the men again and the sight was enough to make me drool. "Who wouldn't be?"

"That's my girl." Cara was grinning at me like we'd been friends since childhood just like her and Katie.

"But I can't make any promises," I started.

Before I could get any further, Katie cut me off with a

wave of her hand. "No one expects you to, least of all them. They know it's on them to show you how it can be." She gave me a wink. "Trust me, you'll have the time of your life being convinced."

Now *that* I could believe. I snuck another peek over at the men and saw that Cole and Declan were heading back in our direction. Girl talk time was over. But I was better for it—my head felt a whole lot clearer and they'd helped to calm some of my nerves.

"What did we miss?" Declan asked, sliding in next to me.

Cole was giving Cara an exaggerated scowl. "Whatever this one said about us, it's not true."

Cara batted her lashes. "I said nothing but wonderful things. Didn't I, Hannah?"

I nodded dutifully. "They were extremely positive. And quite helpful."

At their questioning looks, Cara said, "I told her it was up to you boys to show her how good it could be. Not that I want to know anything about it." She frowned, then flashed them a wicked smile. "Don't let her down, fellas. She's a keeper and I think she'd make a good addition to the family."

Cara and Katie slid out of the booth and went off to find their men, leaving me a blushing, sputtering idiot in their wake.

God, how embarrassing. They must have known

exactly what we were talking about. I ducked my head to avoid their gazes, but Cole placed a finger under my chin and tilted my head up.

"She was right, you know. It is up to us." Holy shit, he was sexy. My eyes were fixed on his lips and that scruff on his jaw. How would it feel to kiss him? "We can stay here, play some pool, have another beer. Or we could get out of here."

Declan placed a hand on my thigh and my attention was drawn to those intense, blue eyes and those broad shoulders. "We want you, Hannah. What do you say, will you let us show you how much?"

Oh holy fuck, there was no way in hell I could say no even if I wanted to. And I didn't want to. I'd been living a nightmare for weeks...months. I'd given up my dream job and was on the run from a man who terrified me. I was desperate for release, and god knew I was so ready for a man-induced orgasm, I could barely sit still.

And now, two insanely hot men wanted to fuck me.

I let myself do what I'd been dying to do in the truck. Placing one hand on Cole's thigh and the other on Declan's, I looked from one to the other. "Show me."

6

ANNAH

The guys wasted no time flagging down the check and hustling me out the door. We left so abruptly I was a little afraid of what people might think. Cara and Katie and their men would surely know why we were leaving so soon after our little chat. But as soon as the thought occurred, I dismissed it. If there was one thing I'd learned about Bridgewater, no one here would judge me for having a threesome with Cole and Declan. Heck, they'd all been pushing them on me at the diner. Katie had even said she'd gotten it on with her men in the back hallway. If they didn't care, why should I?

An odd sense of freedom and disbelief had me stifling a laugh as Declan reached for my hand in the parking lot just as Cole wrapped an arm around my shoulder. What was I doing? This was so not like me. I'd clung to the idea of Brad for so long because he was everything I was supposed to want. Handsome, he had all his hair and a good job. High military rank. A pension. On paper, he looked perfect, but in real life...

Then there were Declan and Cole. While they, too, were handsome—they made Brad look drab and toothsome—had jobs and all their hair, they came as a set. They were both interested in me, both wanted to get me naked. Together. In any other town in America, they'd be fighting each other over me. Here, in Bridgewater, they were working as a team to make me theirs.

Insane.

They guided me toward Cole's truck and helped me up.

Once I was firmly wedged between them, the anticipation grew. I didn't know if I was more nervous or excited, but either way I had a hard time sitting still. How were they going to do this? I knew the possible scenarios for a threesome. I'd read books, seen bad porn. If they were going to take me together, I had three holes for two cocks, so...I clenched my bottom at the idea of double penetration. I wasn't ready for that. My bottom? Nothing had ever gone in there before. Would it hurt? Of course, it would. But Cara and Katie seemed perfectly fine and they never mentioned any challenges in that department when they gave me their pep talk. There was no way in hell their men weren't interested in butt stuff. I was missing something, especially in that department, and I was sure the men would help me figure it out.

It seemed I wasn't the only one who could hardly wait. The silence in the truck only added to my nerves and I bit my lip to keep from babbling like an idiot, which I had a tendency to do when I was nervous. I wanted to ask them about the logistics of the whole thing, but how did you ask a guy how he was going to fit in your virgin ass? Yeah, that wasn't going to happen.

I mean, I hadn't seen either of them naked, but there was no way either guy was small. No, if their cocks matched their physiques, then...

I clasped my hands together tightly and stared straight ahead. I was doing this. Holy shit, I was really doing this. Even the butt stuff. Somehow.

Declan reached over and unknotted my hands. Gently taking one in his, he brought it over to his lap and stroked it, massaging my palm with his thumb in a move that managed to ease some of my nerves while ramping up my senses. God, just that simple touch was enough to make my breathing shallow and my belly clench in anticipation.

When he finished, he placed my hand on his thigh, silently encouraging me to continue my exploration that I'd started back at the bar. He didn't have to tell me twice. My hand seemed to have a mind of its own. I stroked his thigh and watched out of the corner of my eye as his erection hardened, bulging against his faded jeans. My mouth went dry. Holy shit, I was right. He was big. And long.

Oh god, my panties were totally ruined.

He took my hand and slid it up further. I didn't pull away, my curiosity getting the better of me. I wanted to feel him, how big he was. With his hand over mine, I slid over his cock and he hissed out a breath. A flicker of triumph shot through me. It had been a long time since I'd felt so powerful with a man. But I had two men with me.

It was Cole's turn. Leaving my hand on Declan's cock, I reached out with the other for Cole and touched his upper thigh cautiously. "Should I touch you too?" I asked.

"Easy, darlin'," he said. His voice was a low growl. "I've got to get us to Dec's in one piece and what you're doing is enough to make me come right here and now."

"Really?" I asked, surprised. I bit my lip to keep from laughing. God, it felt good to be wanted.

"You can touch us all you want when we get there," Cole said, his voice rough with need. "We're yours for the taking."

I stopped breathing for a second as all the possibilities raced through my mind. Oh shit, I hadn't even realized how dirty my fantasies could be until they were given free rein.

"But it goes both ways," he added.

Declan leaned over so his lips were close to my ear. "You're ours for the taking," he said. "And we're going to touch you everywhere, until you're begging for mercy."

Oh sweet Jesus, I nearly whimpered at that. Yes. Yes! Make me beg.

"We'll be there soon," Declan said reassuringly. Apparently, my desperation was easy to read.

Cole reached for my hand which was resting innocently on his knee. "In the meantime, why don't you show us how you like to be touched."

My mouth fell open as I looked from one man to the other. Oh no. I couldn't. I was the opposite of an exhibitionist—when Brad and I would have sex, it was always in the dark, under covers and I hadn't been as turned on as I was right now in all the times we'd been together. Combined. I couldn't possibly—

"That wasn't a request." Cole's voice had grown hard, commanding. Maybe it should have scared me, since Brad would make demands that scared the shit out of me, but it didn't. There was no coldness there, no cruelty.

Still. I swallowed, lifted my hands and folded them in my lap. "I'm sorry. Don't think me a tease. I'm...I'm afraid."

The truck slowed a little, but Cole kept his eyes on the road. "Are you afraid of *us*?" he asked.

Was I? Was this fear of them?

"I don't know you," I started. "While everyone has vouched for you and you've done nothing to make me scared, I can't help it."

"Yet you just had your hand on my cock. You're not afraid," Declan said, contradicting me. "There's something else."

He had a point. I hadn't been afraid to get in the truck with them. I hadn't been afraid when I was touching Declan, or even when I tried to do the same to Cole. It was Cole's words that had set me off. No, it was his tone. "I don't like it when I'm not given a choice."

"You mean when I told you what to do, when I told you to show us how you touch yourself," Cole replied.

I nodded.

"What do you think would happen if you said no?"

That they'd be mad. Or worse. I couldn't tell them that. "That you'd...God, I don't know."

But I did know and refused to say.

"You didn't do it, which means you were saying no. At least without words."

I thought for a second. "I guess that's true."

"That's right, darlin'. And what happened?"

I looked up at Cole. He was watching the road, but his gaze met mine for a second. I didn't see anger. I didn't see fury building. I saw, god, earnestness.

"You listened to me. My concerns."

Cole took my hand, lifted it to his mouth and gently kissed the knuckles. "I like to be in charge, if you hadn't already noticed. Especially in the bedroom. I'll never, ever, make you do something you don't want to do."

He kept my hand in his, but I knew I could pull it free at any time.

"That goes for me, too," Declan added. "No matter what you might think—and feel—otherwise, we aren't driven by our cocks."

"We're driven by you," Cole replied. "Let me ask you this. Are you wet for us?"

I bit my lip, then nodded.

"Good girl. Now if I get all dominant with you, it's because I want you to forget about everything but what we're doing together, about what feels good."

"Like BDSM."

Declan took my other hand, kissed it. Now both men held my hands as I sat between them.

"If you're into bondage, we'll be more than happy to tie you to the headboard. Dominance is definitely something we like," Declan continued, listing all the parts of the acronym BDSM. "I'm not much into doling out pain and I highly doubt you're a masochist."

Was I into pain? "Yeah, no."

"So let's try something, keeping in mind we'll stop whenever you want," Cole said. "Okay?"

"Okay," I replied.

"Be a good girl and show us how you touch yourself," Declan said, releasing my hand. He was repeating Cole's earlier words. The tone was a touch different, but I didn't miss his "in charge" personality.

When I turned to Declan, his small smile was encouraging but he was waiting for me. They wanted to see what made me hot. That made them good, unselfish lovers. Right?

Brad had done a number on me. Destroyed my confidence, made me think all men were just like him. I'd escaped him to live my life, but I was letting him control me still. Cole and Declan were not like Brad. At all. It was unfair of me to compare them. When they were bossy and all alpha male, I liked it. I really liked it. And knowing they were doing it because it was fun—and hot—I wanted to give over to it. To what I really wanted, and that was them.

My breathing was ragged as I slowly hitched up the

hem of my dress. I was sure my face was bright red as I slowly exposed myself, but the cab of the truck was too high for anyone to know what I was doing. As if he could read my mind, Declan added, "No one else can see you, Hannah. Just us. We'll never share you with anyone else."

That eased my mind, knowing what we did was private. Special. Spreading my legs slightly, I pressed my fingers against my soaking wet panties and bit back a moan.

Oh fuck, I was really close to coming. How was that possible?

Cole made a tsking noise. "Sorry, darlin', that's not gonna do."

I froze, my hand stilled as I flicked my gaze up at Cole, who winked.

Declan explained. "We want to see exactly what you're doing, where you're touching, sweetheart. Lose the panties." His tone was kind, but stern. I didn't think it was possible to get more turned on but his command did it. They'd eased my mind about that, which made it okay for me to like them all bossy. I shouldn't like it after Brad —who hadn't made it sexy at all—but I did, perhaps because they weren't Brad. I sighed. Enough about Brad.

I lifted my hips and pulled my panties down to my knees.

"Spread your legs," Cole said.

I did as I was told and was rewarded by their groans of pleasure at the sight of my wet pussy. It wasn't even eight and the sun hadn't gone down yet. They could see me clearly. They could see everything.

"Show us." Declan's voice was hoarse.

I moaned softly as my fingers found my clit, closed my eyes. This was so wicked, so dirty. I circled my fingers over the sensitive nub, shifted my hips, whimpered. I worked myself in the familiar circular motion, but I was wetter than I'd ever been and the sound of it filled the cab of the truck along with my ragged breathing. Knowing their eyes were on me made me hotter, made me close to the brink. I continued to play as Cole drove. "I can't. If I do, I'm going to come."

"We've got you," Cole said. The truck came to a stop and the men started moving. Only then did I open my eyes as Cole slid out of the driver's side and Declan shifted so he was facing me. "Lie down and spread your legs."

"What?" I asked, startled and confused, but Cole undid my seatbelt, then eased me down so my head was in the driver's seat. What the fuck was I doing? Before I could take that thought any further, Declan slid from the truck so he stood in the open door, hooked my knees and pulled me toward him. I gasped at the bold action, but then cried out when he did something even bolder. He put his hands on my knees and buried his face between my thighs. As his tongue licked my pussy, all I could say was, "Oh god, oh god," and clamp my thighs against his ears.

7

ANNAH

He was good. Really good at this, flicking my clit with ruthless precision. With my fingers tangled in his hair, I came so hard I couldn't see or hear anything but my own pleasure.

When I finally opened my eyes, I found myself looking up upside down at Cole's extraordinarily smug smile. I lifted my head and saw Declan grinning at me, using the back of his hand to wipe his mouth. To wipe my arousal off his face. I started to scramble upright and both men reached out to help me. In an awkward maneuver, I started to tug up my panties that dangled about one ankle, but Declan snagged them, worked them off then stuffed them in his shirt pocket.

My mouth fell open when I realized he had no intention of giving them back. I wasn't just bare assed, but I was bare assed where someone could have driven by.

"Oh god, I did that on the side of the road. Anyone could have seen us."

Declan grinned, clearly pleased with his oral skills. "We're in my garage."

I pushed up onto my elbows, then upright. We *were* in a garage and the door was closed. Light from a window on the side wall and the bulb from the opener offered plenty of light. When had they closed the door? I'd been so far gone I hadn't even noticed we'd gotten to Declan's house, let alone inside the garage.

Sighing in relief that I hadn't had a guy eat me out on the side of the road, I took stock. I felt good. Really good. My fingers still tingled and I was hot all over, but I couldn't remember feeling so relaxed. I couldn't help the grin that escaped. Holy shit, I'd needed that. "That was, um...thank you."

Declan laughed off my thanks. "You don't need to thank me. It was my pleasure. I've been dying to taste that sweet pussy of yours since the first time we spotted you at the diner."

Cole added, "You have no idea how many times I

wanted to lift up the skirt of your uniform and eat you out."

"Oh." That was all I could think of to say. One little orgasm and while they were still gentlemen, they weren't holding back any longer. This was the real Cole and Declan. Handsome, bold, slightly arrogant, very demanding and very, very thorough.

I might have been out of my element with these two —I never imagined what we'd just done—but I was determined to enjoy every second. And I'd certainly enjoyed the last few minutes. More than I'd ever had in my life. And that had just been Declan's mouth and we had all our clothes on. Except for my panties.

This little fantasy wouldn't last long and now that I knew what they could do, there was no way I'd let my inhibitions and hang-ups keep me from reveling in my one and only chance to live out my dirtiest daydreams. And I had no doubt they could fulfill every single onc, including some I never knew I had.

Declan leaned in, pulled me out of the truck and tossed me over his shoulder like I weighed nothing. I didn't know whether to laugh or shout in indignation, but laughter won, especially when I caught sight of a grinning Cole following behind us.

Declan gave my ass a smack as he took me inside and up to the bedroom, taking the stairs two at a time. "You're ours for the night," he said as he set me down in front of a king-sized bed.

I looked up at the dark, brooding hottie and then over to Cole, with his handsome, classic good looks. Just a few minutes ago I'd told him talk like that scared me, but now, it didn't scare me at all. It made me eager.

I was theirs for the night? Yeah, I was so okay with that. I just hadn't known I needed a really good orgasm to figure that out.

"Take off that dress," Declan ordered. While he crossed his arms over his chest, he winked, taking the bite out of the words. Now, I wasn't afraid of his dominance. I reveled in it.

I couldn't help but grin at him as I shimmied out of it, pulling it over my head and saying a silent prayer of thanks that I'd thought to wear my nice black lace bra and panties. Although, my panties were in his pocket so the effect wasn't the same. The way they were staring at me, it didn't seem they minded. Not one, cock hardening bit.

Even so, I felt awkward and exposed standing there in next to nothing while two fully clothed men eyed me unabashedly from head to toe. That awkwardness disappeared quickly as I saw the desire and appreciation that they made no attempt to hide.

"Holy fuck, you're so beautiful," Cole said quietly. He took a step toward me. "Lose those bra, darlin'."

I started to do as I was told but then stopped. I knew what was coming. These guys would make me come again...and again. They were hell bent on making me happy, on showing me how it could be. Not that I was complaining, but there was something I needed first. My mind flashed back on that feeling I'd had earlier in the truck when my hands were on their legs. I'd seen their cocks grow hard and seen the effect I had on them. That feeling was what I wanted right now. I needed to experience my own power first before I let them have full control.

"Wait," I said. To my delight they froze instantly. For all their commands and orders, I was the one who set the ground rules here, just as they'd told me. Their reaction was proof they would never do anything I didn't want them to do. I'd known that deep down, but seeing it with my own eyes was satisfying.

"Is something wrong?" Declan asked, concern written all over his face.

"We told you, we can take things slow," Cole said.

I swallowed down a laugh. Slow was not what I had in mind. I shook my head. "It's not that. It's just...I want to see you first."

That earned me a wicked grin from Cole and a laugh from Declan. "If the lady insists."

They shed their clothes quickly and as they dropped

their jeans and then their boxers, my mouth fell open. "Wow, um...wow."

Holy hell, they were bigger than I'd imagined. Long and thick, their hard cocks just begged to be touched. And when Cole gripped the base of his and began to slowly stroke it, a bead of pre-cum forming at the tip, I licked my lips. I wanted to taste them, to make them come like I had.

In a surprising twist, I realized their concern and then dominance made me bold. I could be myself. No, I could be a new me, a me that didn't shy away from what I wanted. I was passionate and wild, a little dirty too, and I was going to embrace the hell out of it.

When they told me what to do, they were giving me space to forget everything and just flourish, to let my pleasure and desire take over. I gave in to that now, dropping to my knees before them. "Who's first?"

"Whoa, darlin', you don't have to do this," Cole said, eyes dark. Heated. I'd shocked them, that much was obvious. He'd stilled at my bold behavior, but still gripped his cock.

"I do. I so do," I replied as I glanced up at them. They were so big, so powerful and yet gentle. Thoughtful. "I was afraid, but I'm not any longer. One orgasm seems to have helped. A lot."

They both grinned.

"I want this. I want you. Both of you."

Cole growled with approval and Declan stepped forward, grasping his cock and carefully working it into my open mouth. Once I closed my lips around him, he slid his hands into my hair to hold me close.

Oh shit, it had been so long since I'd done this, a little part of me was hoping I hadn't forgotten how. But it turned out sucking a cock was like riding a bike. I moved my head back and forth, taking his shaft in and out, using my tongue to stroke his length and reveling in the sound of his moans. He was like velvet against my tongue, but rock hard. Too big to take his whole length, I wrapped my fingers around the base—they wouldn't close all the way—and worked him as I drew in my cheeks as I sucked.

I heard Cole moving toward me and felt him brush his cock against my cheek, felt the streak of pre-cum. This was hot, dirty and really, really good. Pulling back, I released Declan and took Cole's cock in my mouth, swirling my tongue around the flared head as if it were a lollipop, licking up the salty essence. He didn't even let me take him into my mouth, to feel him slide into my throat, before he pulled back.

"You had your turn, Hannah. Now it's our turn to be in control."

He paused, waited for me to nod, then said, "On the bed. Now."

I no longer panicked at that authoritative tone. I didn't do anything but get wetter.

Declan gently pulled me up and helped me onto the bed. With deft fingers, he unclasped my bra, my breasts falling free. My nipples were already hard, but ached with the feel of the cool air.

"Hands and knees," Cole commanded.

Oh yes. God, the idea of him taking me from behind had me moving quickly. As soon as I did, he knelt on the bed at my side and ripped the wrapper off a condom. I watched the play of abs as he moved, took in the dark line of hair that traveled down to his cock. And that beast.

Was it going to fit? My pussy clenched, eager to find out.

My breasts hung down and my ass was up. Everything was on display and I didn't care. I just needed that big cock of his deep inside of me. Now.

"This is going to be quick, darlin'." He glanced up from sheathing himself, grinned. "Next time, we'll go nice and slow."

Worked for me. "Yes, hurry."

Who was that breathy sounding woman? I couldn't believe this was me. Naked and in bed, desperate and damn eager for two cocks.

He moved behind me, nudging my knees wider with

his own as Declan sat down on the bed, leaned back against the headboard, propped up with the pillows. Taking my arm, he pulled me so my hands were on the bed, but this time on either side of his hips. My mouth hovered directly over his rigid cock. It curved up, just touching his navel. I knew what he tasted like, what he felt like in my mouth and I wanted it again. I wanted to feel his fingers tangle in my hair, guide me as to what he liked. I wanted him to come in my mouth so I could taste him, swallow down every drop.

Cole slid over my folds, then pressed his cock slowly into my wet pussy as Declan guided my head and he slid between my lips.

Cole quickly found a rhythm that was hard and fast, filling me up as I greedily sucked on Declan's cock. I moaned as Cole slid over my g-spot again and again. Declan groaned in reply and tightened his hold on my hair with one hand, cupped and played with my breast with the other.

I was going to come. I was so close, pressing my hips back, meeting Cole's thrusts to take him as deep as he'd go. But it wasn't enough. Somehow, he knew, for he reached around and began to circle my clit with his thumb. I moaned again and this time Declan lifted his hips, thrusting his cock deep into my mouth, thickening, then coming. Looking up at him, I watched as he clenched his jaw, groaned with the pleasure of the hot, wet suck of my mouth. I felt the spurt of his hot cum against the back of my throat as Cole pinched my clit.

I came on a muffled scream, my eyes closing and giving over to the body shaking, heart pounding, breath stealing pleasure.

Cole fucked me, all cadence lost, having given over to his basest need to come. On a shout, he gripped my hip and filled me, his cum captured in the barrier of the condom.

Declan lifted me off his spent cock before pulling me into his arms, our skin, damp with sweat, clung together. He was warm, so very warm and he was hard and powerful, broad and protective when he wrapped his arms about me.

Cole slid from me, moved to the bathroom and returned after a minute. He brought a warm, wet washcloth and gently cleaned me up but I was too spent to care that he was tending to my most private parts.

Finished, he collapsed in a boneless, utterly satisfied heap beside us on the bed. How had I ever thought these two were scary? They were like big, brawny teddy bears. Men who liked to fuck hard and cherish deeply.

After a little while, they shifted me so I was snuggled in between them, my head on Declan's chest and Cole's warm body wrapped around me from behind. A blanket was tossed over us and I gave in to a very sated sleep.

When I woke, it was still dark and the men were

sleeping on both sides of me. Everything we'd done came back in a hot, sizzling instant. Holy shit, what had I just done? I'd slept with Declan and Cole. Not just slept with them, but fucked them. Yes, there was no other word for it. I was such a dirty, dirty girl. Nope. I refused to feel guilty about it. About the ache between my legs. But that didn't mean I should stay here. Fun time was over and so was the one night.

One night, that was all this was meant to be. One spectacular night that I'd be reminiscing about for the rest of my life. We'd all had fun, gotten to know each other in ways I hadn't expected—like the feel on my tongue sliding over the pulsing vein that ran along the length of Declan's cock or Cole's fingers as he held me still so he could pound into me.

Yup, dirty. Filthy dirty. And liberating. I wouldn't be scared any longer.

I moved slowly, easing from the crook of Declan's shoulder and lifting Cole's arm from around my waist. I'd nearly made it to the edge of the bed when I heard Cole move behind me. Next thing I knew, his arm was once again cinched around my waist, keeping me in the bed. His hand cupped my breast, a perfect fit.

"I don't think so, darlin'."

"I, uh, I need to get home," I whispered, not wanting to wake Declan.

"There's no way in hell we'd let you do the walk of shame."

"I don't mind, I'll just—"

He tugged me back so I was lying pressed against him, once again cuddled up between him and Declan, who was starting to stir.

"No arguments," he said, his hand gently roving up and down my arm. "This date isn't over until we drive you home."

It seemed it wasn't going to be now. I relented with a sigh. I supposed there wasn't much harm in extending my fantasy night for a few more hours. At least until the sun came up.

Cole shifted, coming up on his forearm so he was leaning over me. The room was dark, but the glow of the moon through the window allowed me to see his eyes were dark with want, his smile was soft but his voice...his voice was full of promise. "Besides, you can't go anywhere until I've had my own taste."

My sleep-deprived brain didn't know what he was talking about at first. It didn't click until he eased himself down so he was between my thighs, his hands pressing them further and further apart. I felt his warm breath fan over my delicate skin just before he put his mouth on me.

8

ANNAH

The next time I woke up, Cole was sitting at my side, a steaming mug of coffee in his hand and a cocky smile on his face. He wore a pair of loose track pants and nothing else. The view was very appealing. "Morning, darlin'."

I scrambled to sit up, nearly knocking over the mug he held out to me as I tugged at the sheet to cover myself. I mumbled my thanks, my cheeks as hot as the coffee.

His grin grew wider. "You were in an awful hurry to get out of here earlier this morning. You work the lunch shift today?"

I shook my head. "Not until dinner."

His mention of what he'd done earlier had me looking anywhere but at him. Having my pussy licked by a relative stranger first thing in the morning wasn't exactly an everyday occurrence in my life. Actually, that had been the only occurrence. Something told me if I let this go on any longer I'd have no end of early morning orgasms.

Cole made a tsking sound as he gently but firmly pulled the sheet away from the hand that wasn't holding my coffee. "Where did that dirty little mind of yours just wander off to?"

I clamped my lips together. No way was I going to admit that I was reliving the feel of his tongue on my clit. This was supposed to be a one-night deal. I shouldn't be encouraging this any longer, but he seemed to be able to read my mind. His suspicions were confirmed when he slid his hand down my belly and over my pussy. He groaned and so did I, his eyes meeting mine. "Someone woke up nice and horny for me, didn't she?"

I bit my lip. I could try to deny, but what would be the point? He could feel how wet I was and I was growing wetter by the second as his fingers slid between my folds, stroking my clit. Ah hell, who was I trying to fool? I gave him a short nod, shifting so I could move up onto my knees and give her better access.

His smirk was irritating and sexy at the same time. "Say it, darlin'."

"I'm horny." There, I said it.

He slid one finger inside me and I arched my hips instinctively. With his free hand, he took the mug from me before I could spill it all over myself. I only heard as he set it on the bedside table since my eyes had fallen closed, my hips rocking into the gentle slide of his finger.

"Tell me what you want," he said, his lips next to my ear.

I couldn't. I shouldn't. This was supposed to be over. It was day two of a one-night stand. I was already breaking my own rules.

He slid a second finger inside and I gasped. I was going to come, just from the way he was curling his very dextrous digits. Why would I want to argue with him now?

"Tell me," he growled.

"I want to ride you." I was sure my cheeks were flaming red because I'd said such an illicit thing aloud, but his murmur of approval erased any embarrassment.

"Good girl," he whispered. Grabbing a condom from the nightstand, he tugged down his pants enough to free his cock and quickly rolled on the condom. Then he shifted me, pulling me over his lap. He was sitting on the side of the bed, feet on the floor and I was facing him, straddling his hips...and his cock. "You want to sit on this?"

He was teasing me, the corner of his mouth turned

up in that wry smile of his. He easily held me over that hard, long cock so I was close but couldn't take him inside me. My inner walls clenched with anticipation.

"Yes," I whispered. When he still didn't relinquish his hold on my hips, I met his gaze. "Please."

"Good girl," he said again. "I love it when you tell me what you want." He released his grip on me and I eased down, his thick cock stretching my pussy as I took him inside me, shimmying my hips to get him to fit.

Oh god, he felt good. But there was one thing missing. "Where's Declan?"

"Right here, sweetheart." I heard his voice at the doorway. "I see you two got started without me."

I lifted my hips and sank down again, loving Cole's hiss of approval. I saw Declan's hands sliding around my waist from behind and come up to cup my breasts, to tug at my nipples.

This. This was what I'd wanted. To be surrounded by my men.

Not mine, I reminded myself.

"It's time for this, sweetheart."

Declan's hands moved away and he picked up something and held it in front of me. Cole stilled deep inside and I blinked. It was a bright pink butt plug. I'd never seen one in real life, but I knew what it was.

"Um—"

Declan moved it out of my line of sight and I heard the familiar sound of a flip lid opening.

"He won't hurt you," Cole promised, cupping my chin. "You want to take both your men together someday, don't you?"

My mouth fell open to tell them that that they weren't mine, that this was just a one night thing with one more quickie, but I felt the cool, hard tip of the plug pressing against me. There.

"Declan!" I cried as Cole lay back on the bed, took my hand and pulled me down with him, remaining deep inside. His hand cupped my jaw again as he kissed me. It wasn't chaste, his tongue tangling with mine as his hips lifted and lowered in small increments, keeping me eager.

"Just my finger, sweetheart," Declan murmured, circling ever so softly.

It *was* his finger, not the plug and while it had surprised me, it felt good. God, did it. Nerves I didn't even know I had sizzled to life just from the lightest touch. When I saw the plug, I'd thought he was just going to jam it in, but I was wrong.

I lifted my head to take deep breaths. The feeling was intense and new and with Cole inside me, I'd never needed to come so quickly before. Cole was watching me carefully, one hand sliding down my side to my hip, the other moved between us to brush over my clit.

"Oh!" I cried. They were being so damn gentle. No rough play, no demands, just the slightest coaxing and persuasion. How could I tell Declan no when it felt so good?

"Like that?" Declan asked, leaning in and whispering in my ear. "Do you know how gorgeous you are riding Cole's cock? Your nipples are all hard, and your clit—"

"It's all swollen and hard," Cole added. "She's squeezing me like a vice. It's time to come for your men, darlin'."

"Okay," I said, because I was going to do just that. I wasn't going to hold off on the most incredible orgasm ever just because Declan was touching my virgin bottom hole.

Putting my hands on Cole's chest, I arched my back and came on a sharp cry. Cole continued to play with my clit. I began to ride his cock again, using him to stroke every amazing spot inside me. Declan's finger pressed more firmly, then slid into me, stretching me open. It was a sharp bite of sensation and my eyes flew wide, my head lifting to the ceiling. My hair slipped down my back as I came again. Cole was in my pussy, Declan's finger in my ass giving me a taste of what it would be like if they took me together.

They talked to me as I came, but I had no idea what they were saying. I was too lost, too immersed in pleasure to even understand. I just knew that they were there, surrounding me, protecting me, keeping me safe as I let go.

I felt Declan's finger slip from me and I opened my eyes, saw Cole watching me with that little lip curve. When I realized my fingers were like talons in his powerful shoulders, I relaxed my grip, whispered a quick, "Sorry."

"You can leave all the marks you want on me. I'm not going to forget how I got them, that's for sure."

Something cold and hard returned to my bottom. This time I knew it was the plug. "Ready?" he asked.

His hand slid down my back and settled on my bottom, parting me. Looking over my shoulder, I met Declan's gaze. He was waiting for me to say yes, to give him permission. He was very smart, getting me to come from just his finger there, for I couldn't deny that I liked ass play. I'd never come so hard in my life when he was touching me like that. I could tell him no just because it was a little horrifying to admit to liking something so dirty, but we were a little past that now. If many of the women in Bridgewater had two husbands, ass play probably wasn't all that unusual. I was the odd one out.

I nodded and he carefully worked the plug into me. Cole's hands came up to cup my breasts, distracting me from the increasing stretch, and I turned my head back.

"Once that plug is in, I'm going to fuck you. You

soaked my cock as you came and I'm dying here. Hurry, Dec."

I breathed out as he pushed forward, pulled back. I'd seen the plug, it wasn't big, but it felt huge. I winced at the slight burn, then I felt the little "pop" as it slid into place.

"Good girl," Cole said, then flipped me onto my back and I gasped as the plug pressed inward. "Hold on, darlin'. It's my turn to take you for a ride."

I did as he said, curling my legs around his waist as he began to fuck me. There wasn't any other word for it. He wasn't gentle any longer, his need to come was powerful. He felt different than the night before, the plug making it so snug, so much better having both places filled.

The angle of his thrusts made him rub against my clit, which was already sensitive from coming. There wasn't any way not to come again, for my senses were overloaded. Overwhelmed. I milked him as I cried out his name, trying to pull him in deeper still.

He didn't last, coming on a harsh groan.

"I can't wait until we can take you together, sweetheart. This waiting is killing me."

Declan's voice stirred me and his arm banded about my waist, scooping me up off Cole's cock to stand right in front of him at the side of the bed. I felt Declan's clothes along my back. Cole sat up and brushed a thumb idly over my nipple, then stood and went into the bathroom, most likely taking care of the condom.

"Bend over," Declan said, his hand at the center of my back pushing me forward, my hands resting on the bed.

I heard him open his pants, the sound of a condom wrapper opening. I didn't move. "I love the sight of you like this. Bent over and waiting for my cock, pussy all used by Cole and ready for me, the plug in your ass."

God, I wasn't embarrassed by his talk. No, I was aroused and I shifted my hips because I was eager. "Hurry," I whispered, needing him, too. I'd come twice, but I wasn't done. I wanted both of them.

Declan stepped up behind me and slid right in. While the fit was tight with the plug, I was so wet, and as he'd said, ready.

We fucked hard and fast, and he was different than Cole. He moved with a wild abandon while Cole took me with focused precision. They both knew exactly how to make me come, as if they'd been given a manual. Perhaps it was having to watch and wait, but Declan came quickly, but only after he'd used his fingers on my clit to get me off again. He'd said, "Ladies first," before making me cry out and clamp down on him and the plug as I came. I slumped on the bed as Cole removed the plug, used a warm washcloth on me as Declan went into the bathroom.

"I worked up an appetite," Cole said, giving my bottom a playful swat. "Get dressed, darlin'. I hear your stomach rumbling."

They left the room and I got dressed, minus my panties, which Declan had somewhere. My muscles felt like pulled taffy and I couldn't help the goofy smile on my face. I'd been well and truly fucked. Not once, not twice, but hell, I couldn't keep track of how many times. And, it wasn't just simple missionary sex. Oh no. We'd gone so far beyond that, I had a feeling we'd done things illegal in several states. I was a little sore, but I didn't care. I wasn't forgetting the night—and morning—anytime soon.

I headed downstairs to discover that Declan had made breakfast for us. While I knew it was time to go back to my apartment, I was hungry and I didn't want to be an ungrateful guest. And what kind of men were they? Nice, attentive, very skilled, had very large cocks, cooked? There had to be something wrong with them.

As I ate the scrambled eggs, bacon and toast on my plate, I tried to figure out what it was. Once I finished and they were both watching me with satisfied grins, I stood up. As much as I didn't want this to end, my pussy needed a little break and I needed to move on. The night, and morning, of fun was over. I had to let these two go, now, when it was still easy. Well, *easier*.

"Um, well, I probably should get back to my apartment, so thanks for the—"

Of course, they didn't let me go that easily.

Declan took me by the hand. "Thanks? I'm not even going to respond to that, sweetheart." He was quiet as I realized I did sound a little bit insulting. But it had been a one night fling. "You don't have to be at the diner until later today, right?"

I nodded. There was no use lying, they knew my schedule as well as I did.

"Then there's something I want to show you."

9

OLE

It was Dec's idea to take our woman up to the cabin. And she *was* our woman. Last night had done away with any remaining doubts we might have had. While I would have said it was when I slid into her wet heat and felt her pussy squeeze and clench around me, her body adjusting to my claiming, then Dec's, but really, she became ours the second she slipped to her knees, taking us first in hand, then into her mouth.

No, she'd become ours the second we first saw her.

Hannah was the one for us, plain and simple. I thought we'd done a damn fine job of proving it to her, but she'd been ready to do the walk of shame in the middle of the night. I could feel my lips twitching up in a grin at the look on her face when I'd licked that sweet pussy of hers. We'd shown her how it would be and why she should want to stay, naked and between us. But the fact that she'd tried to sneak out of our bed, that she was ready to just say thanks and go home, those were not good signs. Clearly, she still thought of us as a fling and last night was a one-night deal in her mind. That it had just been a wild time. Even after we started to train her ass, told her we'd take her together when she was ready.

I saw nothing wrong with a woman having a fun night in the sack. If she wanted to fuck and suck her way through several orgasms, more power to her. But Hannah wasn't the love-em-and-leave-em type. Not with us. Not with anyone. If she just wanted a night, we'd be the men to give it to her, but she didn't just want that. No, she wanted it all, deep down, beneath all her worries, society rules and other issues we had no idea about. We just had to show her how good it could be. With us. I thought we'd done that, but it appeared not well enough.

Dec and I had our work cut out for us trying to prove her wrong. We'd known she was skittish from the start—clearly, she was trying to keep her past from us, but I had no idea why. Dec was the cop. He was the one who could dig it out of her, and if not, from the computer. This wasn't going to be easy...but it would sure as hell be fun.

"Where are we going?" Hannah asked. She was nestled between us once again in the truck. We'd stopped by her apartment briefly so she could get a change of clothes on our way out of town. While I loved her in her black dress, she needed jeans and sturdy shoes for the backcountry.

"Dec's family has a cabin about an hour out," I told her. "Since you have no car, you don't get out of town to see anything but the few blocks of Main Street. We thought it might be nice to show you some of what Montana's really like."

Dec glanced over at me with a grin. I knew that look. He was happy. So was I. Hell, we still had Hannah between us and we had our clothes on. She wasn't just a quick lay. No, we liked her any way we could get her.

We weren't even trying to hide the fact that we were trying to sell her on Bridgewater. We were like oily used car salesmen trying to make a commission. But the town practically sold itself, as long as one was into the small-town scene. The surrounding mountains didn't hurt either. They were the main draw for the people who lived here. Especially this time of year when the grasses were a bright green and the wildflowers blanketed the meadows. There was so much to do and we wanted to do all of it with Hannah.

"Cara and her husbands will be there," Dec said. "She texted me that they'd spent the night, so you'll have chaperones." Maybe he was trying to put her at ease instead of thinking we might be kidnapping her. Sure enough, she seemed to relax a bit in her seat with that information.

"After last night, aren't we a little late for chaperones?" she asked, amusement tugging the corners of her mouth.

When we pulled up in front of the familiar rugged house—I spent as much time as Dec had at the MacDonalds' place ever since we grew up together—and the smell of the grill had all three of us heading toward the back porch that overlooked the small lake.

Cara's face lit up when she saw us. As Dec and I went over to help Tyler and Mike at the grill, she came bounding over and wrapped Hannah in a hug. We watched them talk and laugh. I was glad she liked Cara. Hell, it seemed she liked everyone she met at the diner. The only people she struggled with was us. Of course, no one else had been trying to claim her either.

"She looks like she belongs here," Mike said, handing us each a can of soda. It was just before noon, not quite time for beers. "Hell, she belongs with *you*. Based on the looks on your faces, you had a good night together."

"That's what we think, too," Declan said, not commenting on how good our night really was. "She's the only one who hasn't figured it out yet."

"Give her time," Tyler said, coming over and slapping

my shoulder. "You know it's always harder for outsiders to accept this way of life than those of us who were born into it. Didn't she just learn about it yesterday?"

Dec and I nodded and I realized I was not a patient man. When the women joined us, I took Hannah by the hand and Dec grasped the other. Hannah blushed but she didn't try to pull away. It was small, but it was a start.

Dec tugged her toward the steps that led from the deck down to the grass. "Before we eat lunch, I was thinking we could show Hannah around the area a bit."

He looked from me to Hannah and she nodded eagerly. "I'd like that."

The three of us set off toward the path that wound around the lake, but stopped at the cabin's dock. The MacDonalds kept kayaks, but they were stored in a small shed until needed. The spot had the most striking view of the mountain peaks, almost purple colored in the sunlight, snow capping the highest ones.

Hannah stopped and took it all in.

"Not what you see in California?" I asked.

She laughed. "Hardly. It's incredible. So peaceful."

A raptor swooped down over the water and she pointed to it as it arced back toward the trees. "So what do you guys do when you come up here?" she asked.

"Well that depends," Dec said, wrapping his arm about her waist, holding her close as we continued to just look. If we weren't having lunch soon, I'd have brought down some chairs to sit in and relax. "During the winter, we go cross country skiing and snowshoeing."

She turned to me. "And during the summer?"

I shrugged. "Anything you want. Kayaking, fishing, hiking—"

"Shooting," Declan finished.

I glanced at him over Hannah's head, knowing he'd said that for a reason.

"We do target practice out in the woods," he continued. "For fun. I could show you how to shoot if you'd like. I showed Cole."

I rolled my eyes. "Says the cop."

She pursed her lips, then frowned. "I'm not really one for guns."

I shot Dec a questioning look, but he ignored me.

He acted too casual as he added, "That's understandable. But some women want to know how to protect themselves. *Most* women in Bridgewater have a handgun in their handbag." He shrugged as if it made no difference, but his motive was plain to me. It was no secret that Hannah was scared of something...or maybe someone. This was Declan's heavy-handed way of getting her to open up. And if she wanted to carry a gun so she wouldn't be so skittish, we'd be first in line to teach her how to use it.

It didn't work. She pursed her lips in thought for a second but shook her head. "Thanks for the offer, but no." Wrapping her arms around herself, she rubbed them to keep warm.

I grabbed her away from Dec, tucked her against my side. "My turn."

She leaned her head against my shoulder, laughed.

"You met in Kindergarten? Seems like you're still there with this sharing thing."

"Some things are worth sharing," I replied, let that sink in. "Come on, let's walk a bit, then head back for lunch."

Dec dropped his attempts to get Hannah to open up, and for that I was grateful. He wasn't a cop at the moment and had to remember she wasn't under arrest. I was as curious as he was as to what had Hannah so closed-mouth about her life before Bridgewater, but pushing her wouldn't get us anywhere.

Lunch was easy going and fun. Listening to Hannah laugh with Cara and her husbands as we ate burgers on the back deck, watching as she pitched in with the clean-up and talked with Dec about his day-to-day duties at the department...the woman fit. Not just between us in bed either. In our lives. Hell, she probably fit in better than I ever had. She looked like she'd been born to be here, with us, in this perfect little corner of the world. If her easy laughter and rare chattiness were anything to go by, she was at ease here. Maybe even at home.

All too soon the afternoon had to come to an end—a

damn shame since I happened to know for a fact that the master bedroom at the cabin had a king-sized bed that would fit all three of us just fine. But Hannah had given us a night and a day and we'd promised to get her back to town in time for her dinner shift.

As if disappointing her wasn't bad enough, I sure as hell wouldn't risk Jessie's wrath if it was my fault she was late. The three of us bid our goodbyes to Cara and her men and climbed back in the truck. Hannah wasn't nearly as talkative on the ride back to town, but she still had that relaxed air about her that was such a change from the nervous persona we'd grown used to.

About halfway back she even relaxed enough to slink down, put her head on Declan's shoulder and fall asleep. I shifted in my seat remembering all we'd done to wear her out.

10

COLE

It had only been a few hours since we had dropped Hannah off at her apartment so she could get ready for her dinner shift, but I was already itching to see her. She was like a drug, addictive. I needed my fix. I parked my truck next to Declan's SUV in the diner's small lot—it had gone without saying that we'd be having dinner here.

I caught sight of her the moment I walked in. She was at a booth toward the back, dropping of Mr. and Mrs. Hardy's meals. Mr. Hardy had been friends with my dad back in the day. The older man still ran his ranch, although his daughter now helped him and would take it over when he retired. Dec was sitting at the counter and I slid onto the seat next to him. We both watched as Hannah came back with a few dirty dishes, put them into a plastic tub. Turning, she noticed the coffee was low and got out the bag to start a new pot. "How's our girl?"

Dec glanced at me with a wolfish grin. "Pretending like the last twenty-four hours never happened."

"Huh." My response was somewhere between a laugh and a sigh. I couldn't say I was surprised. We'd known from the start that she'd resist the idea of something more than a one-night-stand, but now that we knew without a doubt she was the one for us, I was a little disappointed. Last night, hell, even this morning and our time with Cara and husbands, had been incredible. There was a connection that went far beyond chemistry. I knew it. Dec knew it. Hannah knew it, too, but she was refusing to admit it.

She hadn't noticed my arrival and just as I went to call out a hello, plates clattered to the floor at the back of the diner.

"Help, he's choking," Mrs. Hardy shouted.

Everyone in the place rushed into action at once, me and Dec included. Even though he wasn't on duty, he had his radio. I heard him calling for an ambulance as we reached the back booth where Mr. Hardy stood and clutched his throat, his face turning a horrific shade of purple. Panic was in his eyes and he was frantic to breathe, but not a sound escaped. Sam Kane was already behind him attempting to give him the Heimlich, his clenched hands about the older man's middle, pulling back hard as the maneuver required. Sam was strong and even his actions weren't dislodging the obstruction. All at once he passed out, slumping in Sam's hold. He lowered the man to the floor, but we stood around, not knowing what to do now.

Shit, I'd never felt more useless in my life and I was sure everyone else felt the same way. I ran my hand over my hair as I stared down at a family friend in trouble. There was nothing we could do until the ambulance arrived except pray that it wasn't too late. I knew CPR and the Heimlich, and if the airway wasn't open, there was no way to save him.

Mrs. Hardy had her fingers over her lips. She wasn't crying, but she appeared too stunned to do anything but stare.

"Out of my way." I barely recognized Hannah's voice as she pushed me to the side and forced her way through the crowd of patrons who were hovering.

I reached a hand out reflexively to keep her out of the fray. "Hannah, what are you—"

She shot me a glare as she shook me off. "Let me get to him. I can help."

It was shock that had me dropping my hand from her arm. I barely recognized the woman in front of me. Gone was the skittish waitress. In her place was a woman with so much confidence, I swear to god she stood a foot taller. She was the epitome of calm as she kept moving toward the man, not so gently pushing people out of her way like she'd been a bouncer in her former life.

She ordered Sam out of the way and dropped to her knees directly beside the unconscious man's head. She placed a few things on the unmoving man's chest. A straw...and a knife. A sharp little paring knife used to cut fruit.

What the hell?

That was enough to break me out of my frozen stupor and I followed Hannah's path through the bystanders and to Mr. Hardy, Dec right behind me. By the time we reached her side, she had her fingers on his carotid, then slid them up to feel the front of his throat near his Adam's apple.

"Hannah," Dec said. If she heard him, there was no sign of it. Her expression was focused on her task, her lips set in a thin line.

Apparently she'd found what she was looking for. Keeping one finger on his throat, she reached for the knife. I moved forward, ready to grab her arm if need be. "Hannah, what the hell are you doing?"

When she looked up, she was calm—calmer than

anyone else in the diner. Her gaze met mine. "I'm saving this man's life. If you don't want him to die, you'll back off."

She was serious. I found myself taking a step back as her words sank in. I glanced over at Dec and saw the same shock on his face, but he didn't try to stop her. We watched wordlessly as she slowly but confidently put the knife to his neck, pressed down and cut a slit.

She didn't seem to notice the gasps and little shrieks of horror from the those who were crowded around her. Calmly and with steady hands, she used a finger to open the cut, grabbed the straw and inserted it in the small hole.

Leaning over she breathed into the straw, and the effect was immediate. Through his plaid shirt, I could see his chest rising, just a touch, enough to prove air was getting into his lungs. Hannah placed bloody fingers on his neck, felt for a pulse. He must have had one because she didn't start CPR, just continued her rescue breathing.

Paramedics hurried into the diner with a stretcher as those damn bells over the front door jingled wildly, breaking the tense silence that had descended over the crowd as they'd watched the new waitress save a man's life.

"All right everyone," Dec said, his voice loud. "Let them through. Hurry, please."

The crowd backed away, allowing the paramedics to

get to Mr. Hardy. Seeing her giving him breaths through the straw, one of them pulled a piece of flexible tubing from their bag. Hannah slid back on her knees to let the woman swap the drink straw for the sturdier version as the other paramedic hooked up the oxygen and began using the familiar squeeze bag to give him the air he needed. I listened as Hannah gave a report to the male/female EMS team. She didn't sound like a First Responder. Hell, she didn't even sound like a paramedic. She sounded like a doctor. Acted like one, too.

Dec and Sam helped lift Mr. Hardy onto the stretcher as the paramedic continued to bag him. They didn't linger, quickly wheeling him out of the restaurant with a stoic Mrs. Hardy right with them, but my eyes never left Hannah as she stood and watched them leave. Dec went with the paramedics, too busy now in cop mode to figure out what the hell was going on with our woman.

After they left and the patrons started filing back to their tables, Hannah bent down to retrieve the knife and started cleaning the blood off the floor with a rag that Jessie gave her. Her fingers were stained, too.

Seeing this other side of Hannah—it threw me. She was either a paramedic or a fucking doctor. No way some average person knew how to do what she just did. She'd said she'd gone to Stanford, but nothing more. Obviously, there was a whole lot more.

I didn't know what to make of it, just that she'd been

hiding this part of herself from us. A very big part. Why would she do that? What had she done to make her want to keep it a secret? What was her agenda? She'd lied, or at least lied by omission and I couldn't stand that. Just like Courtney, my bitch of a stepmother, this woman had been faking it with us from the start, pretending to be something she wasn't.

She'd been playing us for fools.

I joined her on the ground, my hand on her arm, the grip firm. She looked down at where I touched her and then back up at me, her eyes wide with surprise. I couldn't have kept the anger out of my voice if I'd tried. "You're no waitress," I said. "So who the hell are you?"

She jerked back, scrambling to her feet, the bloody knife limp in one hand, the red stained rag in the other. I stood, too, and she backed away from me so quickly, she bumped into an empty table, scattering silverware. "I—I'm Hannah Lauren."

Her eyes were wide and slightly pleading, as if she could get out of answering questions by playing the damsel in distress. She may have saved the man's life, but she'd messed up. Given herself away. I'd known women like Hannah—beautiful and too smart for their own good. Clearly, she had a plan—she was playing some sort of game with us. Why else would she be keeping so many secrets and lying to us about her past? "What are you up to? What do you want from us?"

My worst fears threatened to consume me. This was exactly what I'd been trying to avoid since my father got taken for a ride by my stepmother. I should have seen it coming. Hannah seemed too good to be true—sweet, smart, gorgeous. Of course, she was up to something.

A new thought ripped through me, making me see red. Maybe she'd been screwing with us all along. She could be a grifter, for all we knew. Hell, she could have fucked us just to get her hands on our money. On my ranch. "Is that why you slept with us last night? Did you think you could get something out of it? Ride my dick and get me to give you whatever you want?"

Her eyes grew wide and she wiped her still-bloody hands on her white apron, leaving red streaks in her wake. "I don't want anything."

Liar. She'd been evading the truth from the start, so how the hell could I trust her word now? I took a step closer and leaned down so she had to look me in the eyes. I saw the flare of fear in her green gaze. "I can't condone liars, Hannah. I don't know what you're up to or why you're really in Bridgewater, but you're not going to get away with it, whatever your game is."

11

ANNAH

I hadn't heard from Declan or Cole in the twenty-four hours since the emergency. What should have been a great moment—someone had called Jessie and let her know the man was going to be fine—had rapidly turned into something terrible. I was glad I'd saved the man's life, of course, and for a moment there it had been nice to feel that rush of adrenaline again, the knowledge that I was in the perfect position to help someone. That's what I'd been trained to do, to help people. But that fleeting sense of euphoria had come crashing down after my run-in with Cole.

I hadn't expected his harsh reaction but, at the same time, I couldn't entirely blame him. He and Declan had been straightforward with me from the start. Honest. They'd made it clear that they wanted me, and not just for one night. They'd wanted me to be the one. Their wife.

I'd known it, known the depth of their intentions, but I'd still assumed it was just a roll in the hay. A quick, hot romp with two cowboys. Or, for them, a wild night with the new waitress. Nothing more. But Cole had been angry. No, furious. If he'd just wanted a quick fuck and nothing more, he wouldn't have cared, wouldn't have hated me so much now.

And if I didn't care for the two of them more than I ever imagined, I wouldn't be so upset. I'd hurt him. Not intentionally, but I had. He thought me conniving or a gold digger. Or worse. I'd ruined something really good all because of Brad.

Damn him!

My chest ached and I fought back bitter tears. I'd wanted to tell Cole the truth yesterday, but how could I? If word got out that I was here and Brad found me...it wouldn't just be me in danger. He'd target Declan and Cole, too. Jessie, even.

I wiped off an empty table with shaking hands. The unfairness of it all made me want to scream, but I had to keep my emotions under wraps. I was the object of enough scrutiny as it was, thanks to that impromptu tracheotomy. Jessie had been giving me odd looks ever since, not to mention the gawking stares from my customers.

Word spread quickly in Bridgewater, and a makeshift operation on the floor of the town's favorite diner? I was pretty sure the news of what had happened spread across the entire town before the ambulance had left the scene.

I'd barely slept a wink, reliving everything. The wild night, the following morning, the picnic, the trach, the harsh look on Cole's face. Even in my dark bedroom with my eyes closed, I saw it all clearly. Heard his harsh words.

Is that why you slept with us last night? Did you think you could get something out of it? Ride my dick and get me to give you whatever you want?

Exhausted, I tried to keep a smile on my face during the lunch rush but it had gotten harder and harder as the hours passed. It became increasingly clear that Declan and Cole wouldn't be coming, wouldn't be smiling and flirting with me. Wouldn't be asking me out again. I'd been dreading seeing Cole again...but I was eager to see him at the same time, to see him wink at me and give me that wry smile.

No. I wasn't going to see that again. He'd been so angry—and so sure that I'd had ulterior motives. I felt sick just knowing he thought I'd slept with them as some sort of game. Did Declan think that, too? I had no way of knowing and much as I wanted to explain everything, I couldn't. I needed to keep them safe. My hands were tied.

I lingered over the tabletop, scrubbing at the surface well after it was clean. I couldn't bring myself to face the other patrons until I'd gotten my emotions under control. I shouldn't have been this upset over losing the affection of two men I barely knew. It was supposed to have been a one-night stand, after all.

Except that it hadn't been. Oh, I could tell myself I'd just been in it for fun—for the novelty of it—but I'd have been lying to myself. Because I'd grown to like those guys. More than just like them, if I was being totally honest. There had been a connection between the three of us from the start and sleeping with them had made it that much more real. It had solidified what I'd already been feeling. That what we had was more than a fling... or at least, I'd started to hope it was.

Those two men had been kinder to me than anyone I'd ever known. The way they looked at me, cared for me...it was so different from my relationship with Brad, there was no comparison. It could have been the real deal.

But, now I'd lost their trust. Clearly, whatever connection we had was broken. Maybe that was for the best. I had to focus on staying hidden from Brad—that was all that mattered. Once he was out of my life for good and I knew I was safe, that everyone around me would be too, then I could focus on finding a new relationship. But in the meantime, I couldn't drag anyone else into my mess. No one deserved that, least of all Cole and Declan.

"Girl, if you scrub any harder you'll ruin the finish." Jessie was laughing as she said it and I turned to give her my best imitation of a smile.

"Sorry, guess I was a little distracted."

Jessie's smile was understanding, as if she had some idea of what I was going through. She patted one of the bar stools in front of the counter as she went behind it to restock the sugar packets for the dinner crowd. "Have a seat. Your shift is almost over and you look exhausted."

I couldn't argue there. I wanted to throw the covers over my head and sleep for a week, but knew the problems would linger.

"What you did yesterday..." Jessie shook her head and placed a glass of water in front of me. "That was incredible."

I looked down at the glass, unable to meet her eyes. She hadn't outright asked me how I'd known how to perform a tracheotomy on-the-fly but the question was hanging out there and I knew she was dying to know. That was the funny thing about this town—while they lived for gossip, they still respected a person's privacy. But I supposed I owed it to her to give her something. After all, she'd taken a chance on me with the job and the apartment. Vouched for Cole and Declan. Still staring down at the water glass, I mumbled, "I've had some medical training."

She gave a snort of laughter. "Yeah, I figured. What I can't work out is what you're doing working here as a waitress if you have a background in medicine."

Again, it wasn't a question so I wasn't compelled to answer. To explain that would mean telling her everything and that was too dangerous.

After a brief silence, Jessie seemed to accept that I wouldn't be offering up any explanations anytime soon. Instead, she changed the topic. "You know Robert Murphy is planning to retire soon."

I glanced up at her, her hands deftly lining up the little white packets then shoving them in a plastic tray. "Who's Robert Murphy?"

"The town doctor." She did a terrible job feigning innocence as she stuck the box of extras back under the counter. "He happened to mention that he's looking for some part-time help at the office until he finds a replacement."

Bridgewater needed a new town doctor?

"Oh really?" I tried not to sound too interested, but my mind was already leaping ahead to the possibilities.

What if I took over his practice? I could have my dream career and still stay in Bridgewater with Cole and Declan. Assuming they still wanted me. No, they didn't want me. They weren't at the diner, were they? It was over. It was a fling, just as I'd wanted. Some of my excitement faded at that thought.

"Robert mentioned that you might be a good fit," Jessie continued, checking the salt shakers down the line of the counter, grabbing one that needed to be refilled.

I looked up in surprise. "He did? When was that?"

Jessie grinned. "At breakfast. He comes in most mornings for his egg white omelet. You've never met him because it's not your shift."

I couldn't help but laugh. "I knew word spread quickly around here, but I can't believe a man I've never even met heard about it in less than a day and wants to hire me."

Her eyes widened. "Heard about it? What you did? Young lady, didn't you see?"

I frowned. "See what?"

Jessie bent down to reach under the counter. "I figured you saw it or I would have shown you first thing. I can't believe nobody told you before now."

"Am I supposed to know what you're talking about?"

Jessie straightened and held up a newspaper in triumph. Her smile widened as she handed it over. "Check it out. You're famous."

My stomach sank before I even saw it. I could hear the blood rushing in my ears as I reached for the paper with numb fingers, but I knew what was coming. Even so, seeing the front page with my own eyes was still a shock.

Local Waitress Saves Choking Man.

I did a quick scan of the article and saw my name, Hannah Lauren. This couldn't be happening. If Brad was looking for me, and I was sure he was, this would get his attention. He'd be looking for Hannah Lauren Winters and if Hannah Lauren showed up in one of his searches —not to mention a Hannah Lauren who could perform a minor surgery—he'd see it. He'd know.

Oh God, this couldn't be happening. Not after everything I'd done to escape and to start over. And why hadn't I changed more of my name? I'd been so stupid! I'd stayed under the radar so far. No credit cards, no ATMs. I'd done nothing that would have me come up in any kind of financial search. One newspaper article and my shabby attempt at hiding was destroyed. I was smart enough to be a doctor, I should have been smart enough to avoid one dangerous ex.

While I was book smart, Brad was street smart and that was dangerous. Really dangerous. He was going to find me. I choked on a sob and clapped my hand over my mouth to hold it in.

"Hannah?" Jessie said. "Hannah, honey, are you okay?"

I couldn't bring myself to respond. If I tried to speak, I'd start to cry. And once I started, I might never stop. It was over. This new life I'd built for myself—a new life that included two men I cared about—it was time to give it up. Time to start over. I had to leave. I couldn't stay here in Bridgewater where Brad would find me and everyone else.

"I'm fine. Sorry, I am tired." It was hard work to fake a smile, but I did it. I stood. "If you're okay here, I'll go take a nap."

"Sure, honey," she replied.

I went out the door and around the side of the building, taking the stairs to my apartment. I hadn't packed much when I fled California, but I'd need it all, wherever I was headed. East, maybe. Or south, where it would be warmer come fall. I couldn't say goodbye to Jessie, to anyone. I thought of Declan and Cole. Maybe it was for the best that they had gotten over the idea that I was meant to be with them. Especially since I wasn't going to say goodbye. Their suspicions would be confirmed, that I'd only wanted them for a quick fuck. Love 'em and leave 'em Hannah. Yeah, that was me. At least, it was now.

12

OLE

My head was pounding, but that didn't stop Dec from giving me hell. I'd been so pissed after I left Hannah the day before, I'd come home and finished off a bottle of whiskey, something I hadn't done since college. Now I was paying the consequences, not just for the drinking but for the way I'd yelled at Hannah.

Dec had been tied up at the hospital in Bozeman and then work so it wasn't until this morning that I had a chance to fill him in on what happened. We were supposed to go see Hannah at lunch like usual but we started arguing and never stopped.

Needless to say, Dec was not pleased by my less-than-forgiving stance. No, he was fucking pissed.

"I can't believe you told her we were through with her without giving her a chance to explain."

I winced at hearing it put like that. My gut churned and it wasn't from the whiskey.

"I didn't exactly say we were through with her."

His sigh was filled with disgust. "Might as well have." He slammed his palm against the wall and I winced, my head ready to fall off my shoulders. I went to the cupboard, pulled down the Tylenol, popped a few in my mouth and stuck my head under the kitchen faucet to wash them down.

"Jesus, Cole, we're supposed to be convincing this woman that she can count on us. That we can be trusted—"

"*We* can be trusted. What about her? Instead of ripping me a new one, maybe we should be more concerned with figuring out if *she* can be trusted."

The look he gave me was almost pitying. "I know you have your trust issues with women—"

I gave a short, humorless laugh at the understatement, ran my hand over my face, felt the stubble that was one day too long. 'Trust issues' was putting it mildly. "Can you blame me?"

He shook his head. "Of course not."

I knew he was telling the truth. He'd been there

during the worst of it. As my best friend, he'd been around constantly when my dad first met Courtney and brought her into our lives. He'd seen with his own eyes just how fake and manipulative she could be. Worse, he'd watched as my father fell for it. He'd been a sucker, and he ended up paying for it with his life. "I'm not going to repeat my father's mistakes."

Dec nodded in understanding. "I get that, Cole. But there's distrust and then there's just plain foolishness. Hannah is not Courtney. Hell, she's nothing like her."

I opened my mouth to protest but he held up a hand to silence me. "Do you really think she came here, to Bridgewater of all places, because she was looking for some guys to swindle?"

Crossing my arms over my chest, I glared at my best friend. When he put it that way...

"And if she was here to con people, what's she doing saving some choking man with a tracheotomy on the diner floor?" His voice rose in frustration.

"Maybe you have a point," I said, grudgingly. My mouth felt like a rat had died in it. I went to the fridge, found the carton of OJ and guzzled some down. I wasn't pissed at him. I was pissed at myself. I wiped a hand over my lips. "But she's still hiding something."

Declan gave a weary sigh, dropped into one of my kitchen chairs, stretched his legs out. "Of course, she's hiding something. We knew that from the beginning.

She was skittish, nervous with us, and not because both of us want her. At this point, all we know for sure is that she's hiding medical training—not exactly damning evidence that she's some sort of gold digger like your stepmom."

"Fine, she's a paramedic or a doctor. Nurse, even. She wouldn't just come here to hide the fact that she knows her shit. What's she really hiding?"

Guilt was nagging at me as his words hit home. Deep down I'd been coming to the same conclusion but sometimes my hatred for Courtney had a way of clouding my judgment. Even with her living in Florida with my dad's money, she continued to fuck with me. But this time, it was my doing, because I hadn't let her shit go. I had a sick feeling in my gut...like I'd made a horrible mistake. I couldn't blame what I'd said to Hannah on the whiskey.

"I don't know what it is, but something tells me she's scared." Declan shook his head. "Haven't you noticed the way she jerked away from our touch when we first met her? Or the fear in her eyes when she'd first arrived?"

I had noticed. We both had. We'd even talked about it. But I'd forgotten all of that the day before in my anger at being played for a fool. Now, I realized I hadn't been played. I was just a fool.

Shit. I owed Hannah an apology. I just hoped I wasn't too late.

My phone cut off the rest of our conversation. I grabbed it from the coffee table. "Jessie? Slow down, what's going on?"

Dec came into the room, leaned in to try and hear what she was saying.

She told me to get down to the diner—said I needed to talk to Hannah, whatever that meant. I hung up and recapped for Dec as I grabbed my truck keys and headed to the door. When I realized I had no shoes, I swore and I went to find them.

"Want me to come with you?"

I shook my head, dropped onto the bench in the mud room, worked on my first boot. "I need to apologize on my own. This is probably Jessie's way of getting me there to do just that."

He laughed. "All right, then I'll head to the station. If Hannah needs us, let me know."

I promised to do that and we both took off. Jessie had been so vague, I was half convinced that this was just her way of meddling. But on the off chance that she wasn't exaggerating, and Hannah really was upset, I pressed my foot to the accelerator and sped all the way there.

When I got to the diner, it was nearly empty. The lunch crowd had left and it was too early for dinner.

Jessie met my gaze from behind the counter where she was pouring a customer more coffee, then pointed toward the ceiling. Turning around, I went back out and around the side of the building. I took the steps to Hannah's apartment two at a time. My head still pounded, but I would live. Before I could knock, the door opened.

She stopped, wide eyed with fear at the sight of me. She wore a pair of jeans and a simple white t-shirt, sneakers. She had a small bag in her hand, as if she was going somewhere. Somewhere far.

"Hannah." As I spoke, I reached out to touch her arm but she gasped and flinched, nearly toppling back into the apartment's living room as she scrambled to get away from me.

Ah shit. The fear in her eyes was unmistakable. I brought my hands up, palms facing forward like I was under arrest. "Easy, darlin'. It's just me."

Some of the tension seeped out of her, but the wariness remained in her eyes and it was killing me. Guilt gnawed at my gut. I'd been such an ass. She wasn't out to get us or trying to play us for fools. I'd let my issues with that bitch of a stepmother cloud my judgment and nearly lost us the love of our lives.

Dec had been right—this woman was running scared. And she was running.

She dropped her bag to the floor with a thud, turned away from me. I followed her in and closed the door behind me, but careful to give her a little distance. "Hannah, I'm sorry. I didn't mean to be so rude to you yesterday. I jumped to all the wrong conclusions and I apologize."

She looked over her shoulder at me, blinked a few times and her eyes started to focus on me. That was a good sign, at least. I couldn't take seeing this feisty independent woman looking so scared. Someone was after her. I knew that now. Could see it as plain as fuck.

Whoever had done this to her would have hell to pay. But first we had to help our woman, starting right now.

I reached out slowly to take her hand and she let me. Let me turn her to face me. "You need to know something, darlin'. I may be an asshole sometimes and Lord knows I have a shitty temper. You, me, and Dec— we'll have our fair share of arguments, but neither of us would ever lay a hand on you."

She was quiet for so long I thought she might never respond. When she did, her voice was soft and sweet. "So you still think there's going to be a 'you, me, and Dec?'"

I grinned at her and she gave me a shaky smile in response. "Darlin', you can't get rid of us that easily. We're not even close to giving up on you. If you're leaving, we're going with you." I leaned in and gave her a soft kiss. "You're the one for us, no doubt about it."

She sighed and the rest of the tension seeped out of her. I pulled her into my arms and she rested her head on my chest. "But you have to tell us what's going on. That's the only way we can help you."

I could feel her nod. "Okay."

"Are you afraid to stay here?" I wondered. She was running and running scared. Of someone in town? Someone from her past?

She nodded. Fuck, no one should be afraid to be in their own apartment.

"Come on, let's go meet Dec and you can tell us both what's been going on."

I called Dec from the truck and he was there waiting for us back at my ranch by the time we pulled up. He didn't say much when Hannah got out of the truck, just took one look at her and wrapped an arm around her, guiding her inside.

Much as we both wanted answers, her comfort came first. She'd been totally spooked when I found her. While she'd calmed down a lot, she'd felt...fragile. Dec made her some food while I drew a bath. It wasn't until she was fed and bathed and sitting between us on the couch that we started asking her questions.

She told us everything—all about her abusive ex and how she went on the run. Dec and I stayed quiet, but my blood was boiling. What I wouldn't give to beat the living shit out of that asshole. I knew Dec was feeling the same way judging by the death grip he had on the mug he was holding. I wouldn't have been surprised if the damn thing crumbled in his hand. But Hannah didn't need our anger, she needed us to listen, so we kept it under wraps.

"I didn't know what else to do, so I ran," she finished.

"I'm glad you told us," Dec said. "Now we can protect you. You shouldn't have to deal with this, with him, alone."

Dr. Hannah Winters. She was a fucking doctor. One who'd gone to Stanford and had just finished up her residency. She'd been working at an ER in LA when her ex had fucked with her. A goddamn doctor, with any kind of social services resource available to her, had been so afraid that she'd run, hid. Hid who she was, even from us. And would have continued to do so except for the choking and the emergency trach.

Hannah shook her head. "I don't want to drag you guys into this. Brad is a real piece of work. You could get hurt—"

Before she could finish, I scooped her up and into my lap, tucked her so my arms were about her. If someone asked if the hold was to comfort her or me, I'd sure as shit say it was to make me feel better. Knowing she was on my lap and safe, that's the only thing that eased my anger. "That's sweet of you to worry about us, darlin', but you've got it all turned around. You're ours to protect and cherish. It's our privilege to take care of you. Your problems are our problems, got it?"

She nodded against my chest and I rewarded her with a kiss. "Tell me, Dr. Winters, how can we take your mind off your worries and help you to relax?"

I saw the smile tugging at the corner of her lips and my heart nearly melted in my chest. It was damned good to see that fear gone and some happiness in its place. Dec moved closer on the couch and one of his hands started stroking her leg.

After her bath I'd left her one of my t-shirts to put on, which fit Hannah like a dress and revealed those long, sexy legs. I heard her breath hitch as Dec's hand reached the edge of the t-shirt and stroked her soft thigh.

My cock grew hard at the thought of all the ways we could help distract her. Judging by the way she started wiggling that ass of hers in my lap, she could feel it. I nibbled on her neck as she and I both watched Dec's slow and steady progress. He was teasing her, tormenting her. By the time his hand reached her pussy she was writhing and trying to find her release.

But that wasn't going to happen so fast. There was one lesson she still had to learn. In one move I flipped her over so she was lying across my lap, the t-shirt ridden up so her rounded ass was bare and so tempting I thought I might come right then and there.

She gasped when I brought my hand down and smacked that ass, watched as my pink handprint appeared.

"When we take control, darlin', it means we want you to clear your brain, to only feel. Control, yes. But you have the power. We're possessive men. With Brad, he wasn't possessive. He was fucking obsessed with you." I spanked her lightly. "Understand the difference?"

"Yes," she replied, sagging against me, beginning to give over.

I spanked her again. "This is for not telling us your problems, darlin'."

When I did it again, harder this time, she moaned. Dec parted her legs as I raised my hand once more. As I brought it down, he thrust his fingers into her pussy.

"Oh god."

"She's so wet," he said. With his free hand he unfastened his jeans as he continued to slowly fuck her with his fingers. He only stopped long enough to pull a condom from his pocket, slip it on.

I gave her a few more spankings, lighter this time, until Dec knelt on the floor and was in position behind her. When he slid his cock into her, I wrapped my arm around her, teasing her nipples through the thin fabric of the t-shirt. I held her in place on my lap as he pounded her pussy.

"Dec, please!" she gasped.

"What do you need, sweetheart?" he asked, hand going to her hip, then to slide between her pert—and pink—ass. "This?"

I knew his thumb had opened her up when she arched her back, thrust her butt out.

"Oh god," she groaned again.

Dec didn't stop, but fucked her with his cock and his thumb. He came quickly and Hannah was still panting for more. She still needed her release—one he had yet to give her—one I would ensure she got. But not until she learned her lesson.

When he moved aside to get rid of the condom, I smacked her ass one more time. "There are no secrets between us." I spread her legs wide and brought my hand down again, this time making sure her wet pussy got a light spanking.

"Is that understood, darlin'?" When she didn't answer right away, I spanked her there again.

This time she wiggled her ass in the air, silently begging for more. Dec sat down on the couch beside me, his cock put away, his pants fixed.

"Yes." It was somewhere between a whimper and a moan and it just about did me in. I moved her onto the couch so she was lying on her belly, her head in Dec's lap. When I moved behind her she lifted her hips and spread her thighs, offering herself. I could see her reddened bottom, her swollen and slick pussy. All of her, and she was giving it to me.

I slid my cock into her in one long hard stroke, making sure she knew who was in control. Wrapping one arm around her, I found her clit with my fingers, making her cry out.

"Cole, don't stop," she begged.

I couldn't have stopped fucking her if I'd tried. She was so tight and wet and with a few more strokes of her clit we came together.

Later, when the three of us were relaxed and content on the couch, our girl between us still in just my shirt, she turned to me with a teasing smile. "I thought you said you'd never raise a hand to me."

I grinned as I reached down and cupped her pussy in my palm. It was still wet and she moaned and wriggled in my arms. Her eagerness for us seemed to be never ending. "A spanking is different. Sometimes you need to know who's in charge. And, you like it."

She moaned her agreement.

"Besides, we had to get it through that thick skull of yours that you don't need to handle all of your problems on your own."

Dec slid a hand up beneath her shirt and tweaked a nipple. We were working in tandem to show her again how it was between us. How we'd always be there, taking care of her. "You need to learn to let go. Let us have control when it comes to taking care of you."

Her breathing grew shallow as his fingers worked her nipples and I could feel her pussy growing wet all over again. I turned to Dec. "Maybe we should show her just how well we can take care of her."

I hoisted her up and carried her to my room, vowing to never stop showing her.

 ECLAN

I was the first one up the next morning and I was glad to have the privacy. Ever since Hannah told us her story the night before, I'd been dying to do a little digging and see what I could find out about the asshole who had her running scared. The best way to beat an opponent was to know where he was coming from and how he thought.

What I found made my stomach turn. A military guy through and through, someone like Lieutenant Colonel Bradley S. Madison was bound to have connections. I was amazed he hadn't found Hannah by now, only proving how under-the-radar our girl had gone. No credit cards. No ATMs, no cell phone. Nothing to make a blip on any searches. Until yesterday.

With her first and middle name in the local paper, it was just a matter of time. At least we knew what was coming. I'd spread the word to Jessie, Sally and Violet Kane. They'd take it from there and the entire town would know to keep an eye out for a stranger, and on Hannah. If we were lucky, Brad would have moved on from this obsession—but I wasn't about to count on that.

I'd been around long enough to know once an abuser, always an abuser. And Hannah had gotten away, which would have pissed him off. He'd have to track her down just to win this battle. He wasn't going to let a mere woman slip through his fingers.

Like Cole told Hannah the night before, while we liked to have control and were possessive, this fucker was obsessive. He'd even come after her at the hospital where she worked. No wonder she'd been so freaked when we went all dominant with her.

It wasn't just Hannah he'd fucked with. He had a history of abuse, from what I could dig up. His ex prior to Hannah had gotten a restraining order against the bastard, which was public record, and I had no doubt she lived in fear. That order was just a piece of paper, not a shield against danger.

Part of me hoped he would come to Bridgewater so I could show him what it meant to be on the receiving end of a beating. Men who hit women were the weakest men alive.

When Hannah and Cole came downstairs, I briefed them over coffee on what I'd found and my plan going forward. I saw her wince when I mentioned telling Jessie and some others so they could help keep an eye out. It was clear she didn't relish the idea of sharing her story, but she didn't fight us on it either. I had to hope this meant she was done running and was ready to fight, especially with an entire town behind her.

"I just wish I wasn't putting you all through this," she said. She glanced down at her mug.

I wrapped my arms around her and pulled her close. "What did we tell you last night? It's an honor and a privilege for us to take care of you."

She rested her head against my chest, but kept quiet.

I gave her ass a light slap. "Do we have to teach you another lesson?"

She laughed at the reminder and the sound had me and Cole sharing a smile. It had been too long since we'd heard her laugh. But hopefully now that her secrets were out in the open, she could have a fresh start with us here in Bridgewater. With everything going on in her life, I knew better than to push her on that topic so soon. First, we'd deal with Brad and then we'd worry about how to make sure our woman stayed here with us for good.

I dropped a kiss on top of her head and started to

pull away. "I'd love to spend the morning with you two, but I've got to get to work."

Hannah perked up. "Can I get a ride back to town? I need to get to the diner early."

"You working the breakfast shift?" Cole asked, knowing it wasn't her normal work hours.

She shook her head. "No, but there's someone who might be there who I'd like to talk to."

Her vague answer had Cole and I sharing another questioning look, but we let it drop. If she was in the diner, we had to believe she'd be safe enough. She looked so damn happy...and a little smug, like she had a secret. I didn't like secrets much, especially with her. But she looked excited this time, not afraid.

It wasn't until we were driving back into town that I got her to spill. "What's this mysterious meeting you're heading to this morning?"

When I looked over I saw that she was blushing and biting her lip. Now, I was really curious.

"It might not pan out..."

I kept quiet hoping she'd confide in me. Sure enough, a few seconds later she turned toward me, one knee on the seat, her face lit up with excitement. "Jessie told me that Dr. Murphy is retiring soon. Seems he's looking for someone to replace him."

As the full meaning of that clicked, it took every ounce of willpower not to pull my SUV over to the side of the road and kiss her senseless. Hope shot through me. Doc Murphy had delivered me. Cole, too. Hell, pretty much anyone born since 1975 in the county. He'd been wanting to retire for a few years now, at least his wife had been. She must have finally put her foot down, and the other husband in their trio had probably taken her side, wanting to move to Arizona to be near their children and grandchildren.

I wasn't too keen on seeing the old doctor leave, but if that meant Hannah would stay...

"So does this mean you're seriously considering staying in Bridgewater?"

She looked down at her hands and then back to me. "I'm thinking about it. I mean, I can't commit to anything yet, not until I figure out this situation with Brad and my career possibilities, but doctors are needed everywhere. Even Bridgewater."

I grinned over at her. All I heard was a bunch of excuses to delay the inevitable. "But you're telling me you'd like to stay here with us?"

She shrugged and fidgeted in her seat. Bit her lip. "If you and Cole still want me." Her voice was soft, as if she worried the answer would be no.

"There's no doubt in our minds, sweetheart. You're the one for us, we're just waiting for you to finally see that."

She didn't respond and I didn't push her. The fact

that she was going to talk to Doc Murphy about potentially taking over his practice was a good sign. She was meant to be ours, we just had to have a little more patience.

———

HANNAH

My talk with Dr. Murphy went better than I could ever have expected. I bit the bullet and explained my situation—not a topic I wanted to repeat but once I got started I found it was easier to talk now that my secrets were out in the open. As the only doctor in town, I was sure he'd heard it all in his long service. My escape from Brad was probably nothing in comparison to some of the things he'd seen. While I'd done my fair share of emergency medicine and felt I had a level head, this man's heart rate probably didn't rise during a harrowing situation.

I got the feeling he was retiring more for his wife than himself—he'd probably rather die on a house call than on a golf course in Arizona, but I discovered she, and her other husband, were ready to move on. Yes, he had a marriage with two husbands and one wife. They were everywhere!

He loved the idea of me taking on some of his patients at his clinic to start. I'd learn the ropes, he'd slowly cut back his hours and the people of Bridgewater would get used to me, although I was infamous in the area after the whole field trach thing. We spent an hour sipping coffee—Jessie came by on occasion to wipe down the clean table next to us, blatantly eavesdropping —and talking about the possibility of me taking over completely before the holidays. They wanted to be settled and have the grandkids in their new house in Arizona for Christmas.

It all sounded so perfect. Almost...meant to be. Except that Brad was still out there.

I was grinning like an idiot all during my lunch shift. Amazing how my perspective on everything shifted after telling Declan and Cole the truth. Maybe I should have told them about Brad and my current situation right from the start. But I hadn't known them then. Trust hadn't come easily. For the first time, I wasn't alone in this mess. I had people looking out for me and men in my life who I could trust. Who would protect me, not beat me. I couldn't miss the way Jessie kept a close eye on me, the way everyone in the diner looked up when the bell on the door jingled. *Everyone* was on alert.

Declan and Cole were picking me up for a late dinner after my shift and I couldn't wait to tell them about my conversation with Dr. Murphy. I looked at the large clock on the diner's wall. I had just enough time to run upstairs to my apartment and change out of my uniform before they showed up. I told Jessie where I was headed and that I'd be right back.

Thick clouds had rolled in, a summer thunderstorm. The sun was blocked and it was dark early. The wind kicked up, swirling my hair into my face. That must have been why I didn't see him—not at first. I was halfway up the stairs when I heard his voice—that voice—below me. "Hannah."

My stomach sank at the sound of my name. I stilled, my hand on the railing. My blood ran cold and my muscles tensed. No, no, no. This couldn't be happening. He couldn't really be here. Not now, when my life was finally starting to come together. Not the first time I hadn't been looking over my shoulder. I'd been so stupid to let my guard down, even for a minute.

Turning slowly, I finally saw him. He stepped out of the shadows and I could see the anger etched into his features. The tension in his body as he slowly climbed the stairs toward me. I couldn't get away. I was too far up the stairwell to jump and his large, looming body blocked my only path of escape.

ANNAH

"Brad, what are you doing here?" The question was stupid, because I knew he was here for me.

"You've been a bad girl, Hannah." The look in his eyes was crazy, unstable. He'd been angry before, but not like this. Veins in his neck stood out, one even pulsed in his temple. He wasn't wearing his uniform now, only a pair of jeans and a black t-shirt. His hair was still military short, his face clean shaven, nothing to hide his roiling emotions. "Did you really think I wouldn't find you? Stupid girl, using your first and middle name. You wanted me to find you, didn't you? You wanted me to chase after you."

I'd never seen him so unhinged. While I'd been afraid he'd hurt me in the past, now I was afraid for my life. He'd come over a thousand miles for me. It had only been yesterday morning when the paper came out. He must have found me online, then got on the first plane. He hadn't waited. No, he'd been waiting for weeks for me to mess up. And now he was here.

Thunder rumbled in the distance. If I screamed would anyone in the diner hear? My feet were stuck as panic made my brain unable to function. Why could I cut a hole in a man's throat without blinking an eye, but completely freak when I was in danger? Should I run upstairs and lock the door or try to call for help? No, he'd follow me in and I'd be worse off alone with him in my apartment.

I waited too long. He reached the step below me and grabbed my arms. The feel of his rough hands, the familiar smell of his cloying aftershave—it was enough to jar me out of my fearful daze.

I screamed and jerked away. Brad was blocking my path down to the diner where there were other people so my only option was up. I had no choice but to go to my apartment. I turned and tried to run but one of his hands caught my ankle and I fell across the stairs, my hands and knees slamming into the hardwood. I scrambled to get back up. My free leg kicked out, made contact with his shoulder.

"You stupid bitch," he growled, stepping higher so he was hovering over me. I could feel him press into my back, trapping me. "Did you really think I wouldn't find you?"

He grabbed a chunk of hair and pulled my head up so his mouth was next to my ear. I cried out again but the sound was weaker this time since my lungs and stomach were pressed against the stairs. The wind kicked up again, hair getting into my face. I couldn't brush it away, my arms trapped beneath me.

"I own you." His breath was hot on my face.

This was what I'd been afraid of. His obsession. Declan and Cole were nothing like this. How they behaved, often like cavemen, was not the same. I saw it now, heard the tone. Felt it. They wanted me, perhaps just as much as Brad did. But they wanted me not as an object or a thing, but as an equal. We were a trio, a threesome, that made each other stronger. Yes, they were bossy as all get out. But I liked it. Heck, I needed them to be that way. It got me out of my head. They took my worries away and replaced it with silence, with peace. With pleasure.

"You're mine and you always will be," he growled.

"No!" I shouted, trying to get him off of me, but it was no use.

"She was never yours and never will be." Declan's voice came from the bottom of the stairs and the sound of it made me sob with relief. A second later, Brad was hoisted off me.

I heard sounds of a struggle but it wasn't until I scrambled to my feet and turned around that I saw Declan and Cole beating the shit out of Brad.

It was...god, a beautiful sight. They were here!

Brad was still on his feet swinging but he didn't stand a chance against my two men. Just the looks on their faces should have been enough to scare Brad off, but he was too much of an asshole to think someone might beat him. They shoved him toward the diner, then through the door. I hurried after them, stumbling once on the steps on the way down.

I let out a choked laugh when I followed them inside. Brad lay sprawled on the floor, blood oozing from his nose and bruises already starting to form on his face. He was still conscious but had the good sense not to fight back.

He was surrounded. Cole and Declan hovered over him, breathing heavily but otherwise they looked unhurt. They weren't done with him. I knew if Brad stood up, they'd fight him some more. Beside them, Jessie held a frying pan raised over her shoulder ready to swing, as if it were softball season. As if that wasn't enough, three of the diner regulars, including Dr.

Murphy, had guns drawn and aimed at Brad's head. Montana really was the Wild West. While I was used to seeing gun shots in the ER and wasn't pro-gun, for once in my life I was happy to see all the weapons.

This bastard would be beaten, crushed, and shot if he so much as moved a muscle.

"Hannah, are you hurt?" Dr. Murphy asked, but his gun didn't waver from Brad.

"No, I'm all right," I said, my voice shaky.

Declan was talking into his radio, but I wasn't listening. I was staring at the cowering, broken Brad.

Cole left the posse to come over and take me into his arms. I hadn't realized I was shaking until he held me close. "You're really not hurt?"

I shook my head. "I'm okay. Or, I will be."

He kissed the top of my head, gave me a gentle squeeze. "You'll never see him again." It felt so damn good to be in his arms, to know I was safe. To know he'd keep me safe. And he had.

Things happened quickly after that. Declan came over and gave me a hug and a kiss before going into full-blown cop mode. After reading Brad his rights, he hauled him out to a police SUV that pulled up out front with flashing blue and red lights. He assured me before they left that I'd never have to see Brad's face again and I believed him. I wasn't sure what the justice system was going to do, but I knew there was plenty of open land to bury a body if he wasn't sent to jail to Declan's satisfaction.

The guns were put away and Jessie placed the frying pan down on the high counter. Everyone settled back to their meals, but news of this incident would be spread across town faster than a wildfire. I was giving the town plenty to gossip about. Jessie got me a mug of tea while Cole tended to my minor scrapes and bruises. He grinned and looked at me with those pale eyes as he said, "I get to play doctor now, although I can think of better ways I'd like to do that."

Yes, I was sure he could think of *much* better ways.

"We're not letting you out of our sight, darlin'," he said.

I liked the sound of that. After everything that happened with Brad, it would be a while before I was comfortable being alone, even knowing Brad was in jail. "Good."

With my one word reply, he took me upstairs and helped me gather some clothes and toiletries so I could take them back to his place. He didn't leave my side the entire time.

While I knew Brad couldn't get me, my hands still shook as I zipped up my overnight bag.

Cole took the bag from me. "Hey." Tilting my chin up he forced me to meet his gaze. "It's over."

The words were a cool, sweet balm. Almost too good

to be true. After living in a nightmare for so long, it was hard to believe Brad was finally out of my life. I didn't have to hide anymore. With one arm about my waist, Cole led me out of the apartment, past my neighbors and friends who'd had my back, and helped me into his truck.

This felt right. Being with him, with Declan. And now I didn't have to hide any longer. I didn't have to be afraid. I had two men protecting me. Possessing me. Pleasing me—at least I hoped they would very soon.

I turned to him with the best smile I could manage. "Take me home."

15

OLE

Hannah was quiet for most of the drive back to my ranch, but I grabbed her hand, held it on my thigh. I would damn well rather drive one handed then let her go.

I stayed quiet, giving her some space to wrap her head around what had just happened. Truth be told, I needed some time myself. It wasn't every day I watched the love of my life face danger and I was still shaken.

Brad. He was a big guy. Thick with muscle and full of anger. Full of anger toward Hannah.

If we hadn't gotten there when we had...

If anything had happened to her...

But it was pointless to go down that road. All those ifs. The biggest one was if he hadn't fucked with her, she wouldn't have come to Bridgewater.

The only consolation was that while he'd hurt her in the past, he wouldn't ever again and we'd be around to make damn sure we kept that promise. I gave her hand a squeeze as I drove us home.

"I'm sorry," I said.

She'd been staring out her side window, but at my soft words, she turned to look at me.

"Sorry? You saved me."

"We weren't there."

She sighed, squeezed my fingers. "You're not always going to be there. I'm not a child that needs a babysitter."

She was right. We couldn't be with her all the time. We weren't like that. Smothering. Controlling. She had to live her life, and I hoped at the end of the day, she'd come home to us.

Dec arrived at the ranch a few minutes after we did. He came into the kitchen where Hannah was sipping her tea and I was watching over her like a fucking mother hen. I'd let her out of my sight. Eventually. Who could blame me?

He sank into a chair as he filled us in on how he'd handed Brad over to his fellow officers to book and process. He scratched his head, his red hair sticking up every which way and looked down at the table. "I couldn't trust myself to deal with that asshole any longer than necessary. If they'd left me alone in a room with that bastard…" He trailed off with a shake of his head. Reaching a hand across the table, he caught Hannah's in his. "Besides, I wanted to get back here and make sure you were doing okay."

She gave him a wobbly smile. "I'm doing great."

I knew that was an exaggeration, but let it go.

"Thank you." She turned to me. "Thank you both. If you hadn't come when you did—"

I shook my head, remembered how it felt when I saw the guy pinning her to the steps. It was only the start of his plans for her. He'd come all the way from California, no fucking way would he just intimidate. No, he'd planned to hurt her. "No point in going there, darlin'."

Yeah, I didn't want to punch a hole in my wall.

She nodded her agreement, swallowed. "So what happens to him now?"

Dec turned on the cop voice I knew so well as he explained what procedures would come next. At the end, he said, "While he's military, what he's done is out of their jurisdiction. It'll be complicated with them getting involved, but long story short, you'll never have to worry about that guy ever again."

He looked up at me and I could easily read his mind. If the law didn't put him away, we'd take care of him. I had no doubt others in town would help, probably even bring the shovels.

Her gorgeous green eyes were filled with amusement. "That's great to hear. But what I meant was, what happens now...with us?"

Dec and I shared a quick look, this time of surprise, before turning back to her. "What would you like to happen next?" he asked. He sounded a little wary, and I couldn't blame him. She'd just been through hell and back. Much as we wanted to take things to the next level, it was very likely she'd ask for some space. Some time. We'd give her whatever she needed, but it would be hell while we waited.

She licked her lips and fiddled with the handle of her mug. "I talked to Dr. Murphy this morning."

I saw Dec sit up straight, a new energy making him look like he might shoot out of his seat at any moment. "In all the fucking insanity, I forgot about that. And?"

And? I had no idea what they were talking about. Why did she need to see the doctor?

Her lips curved up in a grin. "And I could be the town's next resident physician if I want the job. I wouldn't have hospital privileges like he does, but I could get them."

I'd heard that Dr. Murphy wanted to retire, but hadn't thought much about it. Until now. My mouth fell open as the full meaning of that hit me. She wanted to stay here...with us. While we only had a small clinic in Bridgewater, she'd need to be able to admit patients who needed more serious care to nearby hospitals in Bozeman or Helena. I wasn't up on the legalities behind a doctor moving to a different state to work, but I had a feeling it wasn't impossible.

She turned to me and filled me in on what she'd apparently told Dec earlier. By the end he and I were both ready to jump out of our seats with excitement. "So you're staying?" I asked. I had to hear her say the one word.

For a second she looked shy, her gaze flicking from the table to Dec and then to me. "Only if you two are sure that this—"

"We're sure," Dec said, not letting her finish. He grinned.

I got up out of my chair and came around to where she was sitting. Leaning over, I wrapped my arms around her from behind, my lips finding the sensitive spot on her neck that I knew made her shiver. Breathed in her scent. "Darlin', there's nothing that would make us happier. You're ours—now and forever."

She turned her head up to smile at me. She didn't panic this time when I staked my claim. Our claim. "Then I guess I'd better tell Dr. Murphy I'm ready to start right away."

Dec got out of his seat and came around to the other

side of Hannah. "Not so fast. I think the good doctor would understand if you need a few days—"

"A few weeks," I clarified.

He grinned over at me. "A few weeks to recover."

She turned from him to me. "Recover?"

"Mmm," I murmured my agreement as I leaned down to nuzzle her neck, my hands skimming over her waist and hip making her wiggle in her seat. "I'm sure the doctor and Jessie will understand that your men will need some time to take care of you. After everything that happened, you deserve some TLC. Dr. Cole's orders."

Dec was already tugging on her hand, helping her out of the chair. "That TLC starts now, sweetheart." He gave her ass a light slap that sent her in the direction of the stairs. "Now get on upstairs and into our bed."

16

ANNAH

The stern sound of Declan's voice as he ordered me upstairs was enough to make my panties wet. I was easy. I admitted it. But only with them. Maybe it was the rush of adrenaline from earlier, but I was trembling with anticipation as they followed me into the bedroom. Two big men were going to dominate and control me and I wanted it. After Brad, one would think I would avoid all men. The opposite seemed to be the case. I craved these two. Needed them.

I climbed up on the bed readily. I'd long since lost my embarrassment at how eager I was to feel them inside me. Flopping down on my back, I gripped the bedspread in my hands as I watched them come toward the bed, their eyes dark with desire and their cocks visibly straining against their jeans.

They were the ones for me. In this room, I felt safe. Protected. Cherished. Possessed. Perhaps they were obsessed with me, but with these two? I was fine with that. In fact, I was more than eager to see them give in to their obsession because I knew what it would bring me.

Pleasure.

Declan leaned over and started undoing the buttons of my uniform. I groaned.

His fingers stilled. "What?"

"This dress is man repellent. How can you want me in this hideous thing?"

He grinned then. "We don't want you in it. I'm trying to get you out of it."

I rolled my eyes as Cole came to my other side and lifted the hem of it so it was bunched up around my waist. "We'll take you any way we can get you. Haven't you figured that out by now, darlin'?"

I saw the uncertainty in his eyes.

"What?" I asked.

"You know we want you. Long term. We've made that clear. But I think I can speak for Dec when I say we're willing to wait, to be with you any way you want. It's up to you. We just want scraps. Whatever you're willing to give."

I looked between the two. Big and broad. Brawny. Strong. Brave. Cole was laying it all out for me. Yes, they'd said they wanted me. At first, I hadn't really believed it, but they'd proven it over and over that they were there for me, for everything.

I'd strung them along. Yes, I'd gotten naked with them on the first date, but I'd kept my emotions separate. I'd given my body, but I hadn't given anything else. They wanted me. Somehow, they knew I was exactly what they wanted the very first time they saw me. Yet I kept pushing them away.

I was afraid they'd get hurt by Brad. Afraid they'd get hurt by me. That I couldn't get tangled up with two men. I hadn't seemed able to trust what they were saying, that while they wanted me to be theirs, entirely, I'd never said I wanted them to be mine.

They'd told me they wanted me. Over and over and over again. And they were still waiting.

Tears filled my eyes.

"Hey, what's all this?" Declan asked, wiping away one that slipped down my cheek.

"I'm sorry," I said, swallowing hard to will the tears away. While my uniform was ugly as could be, an ugly cry was not something I wanted these two to see.

Cole gave a slight nod, then started to back off the bed.

"No," I said, grabbing his wrist. I sat up and he stilled. I didn't let go. I looked from one to the other, their focus squarely on me.

I didn't want to ever let go.

"I mean, I'm sorry I didn't trust you. I'm sorry I didn't put value in the intentions you had toward me."

"We've said—"

I cut Declan off. "I know. You've said I was yours all along. But I just heard it as possessiveness and not the good kind. I just thought of Brad. I never really believed it. You're talking living together and commitment, mortgages and babies."

Cole perked up at that. "You want babies?"

I wiped my eye, the last of the tears gone. I couldn't help but smile at his eagerness. "Yes, someday."

"That's good, because we want a whole bunch with you. A football team worth."

I slid my hand from his wrist to entwine our fingers.

"That's just it. You knew this all along. I just didn't realize the depth of your interest."

"Maybe we didn't make ourselves clear," Declan said, taking my hand and holding it so we were all connected.

"You did," I confirmed.

He shook his head. "Maybe we didn't say the right words."

"Dec's right. We said everything but the most important three words." Cole lifted our joined hands, kissed my knuckles. "I love you, Hannah Lauren Winters."

The tears returned, but so did a smile.

"And I love you," Declan added. "We might tell you you're ours, but haven't you figured out that we're yours?"

I nodded, sniffed. "Yes, about three minutes ago."

"You can boss us around all you want."

"Even in the bedroom?" I asked, a smile curving my mouth.

"If you want to have your way with me, I'm fine with that," Declan added.

I looked between the two, knew they wouldn't like that all the time. Neither would I. So I told them that. "No, I like it when you have your way with me," I admitted. I looked down at the bed, then up at them. "I love you. Both of you."

The looks on their faces was something I'd never seen before. It wasn't lust. It wasn't anger. It was... adoration. Reverence. Love.

"You want this with us, Hannah?" Declan asked. "Everything?"

I took a deep breath, felt so dang happy. Brad was gone. I had no worries looming. No looking over my shoulder. Only the future.

With them.

"Yes. I want everything with you. But..."

"But?" Cole asked.

"But I don't want babies right now. I'd like to take over for Dr. Murphy first."

They both nodded. "No babies now. That doesn't mean we can't practice." Cole grinned and Declan winked.

I laughed. "Yes, let's practice."

With that, Declan put his hand on my sternum, gently pushed me back. My skirt had fallen back down and Cole worked it up to my hips again.

"Pretty panties," he said, his voice deep. My nipples hardened at the change in tone. Yes, I loved it when they took charge. "Take them off."

17

ANNAH

I did as I was told, shimmying out of them as they watched. I loved having their eyes on me. Knowing these men, these big cowboys were mine, made my heart swell, and my pussy get wet.

Declan spread my uniform wide and undid the front clasp of my bra so my breasts were bare. "Spread your legs for us," he ordered. "Show us that pretty pussy of yours."

"No, of ours." Cole's gaze slid up my body to look at me. I saw the scorching heat and nothing else. "That pussy belongs to us, doesn't it, Hannah?"

I bit my lip to keep from whimpering as I nodded and slowly opened my legs. When they remained quiet and Declan just arched a ginger brow, I spread them wider. I knew I was wet and by the way Cole made a little possessive sound in his throat, he saw it.

"Play with your breasts," Cole said as he climbed onto the bed, unfastening his jeans in the process. His eyes didn't leave me.

"Show us how you like it," Declan urged. I remembered he'd said the same thing before, that first night in the truck and it had scared me. Now, I was scared they wouldn't like what they saw, especially since I'd been wearing the drab uniform. But when I saw Cole's big cock spring free as he pushed down his boxers, I let go of all my worries. I cupped my breasts, loving the way the men couldn't take their eyes off me. I rolled my nipple between my thumb and finger. Cole reached my side and gently moved my hands aside. He took over, leaned down so his mouth covered one hard tip and sucked...hard. His hand cupped the other, played with it.

I cried out and arched my back as he continued to pinch and suck. He wasn't gentle, but I didn't want him to be. This attention made me forget about everything but my men. They were tending to me, taking care of me. Loving me.

My eyes fell closed as I reveled in the sweet torture,

but I was dimly aware of movement at the foot of the bed. I was taken by surprise when Declan grasped my thighs and spread them apart even further until my legs were as wide as they could go. Then he buried his face between them, his mouth on my pussy, licking along the slit, then parting me with his fingers so he could circle my entrance. The scruff of his five o'clock shadow chafed my inner thighs in the most delicious way possible, adding to the sweet pain that Cole was inflicting on my nipples. Declan's tongue lapped at my clit and a finger slipped inside me, curling over my g-spot.

I had one hand tangled in Cole's hair and another holding the back of Declan's head, pressing them both to me as I writhed beneath them, thrusting my hips up for more whenever Declan's tongue left my pussy and moaning my displeasure when Cole released one nipple for the other. Jesus, I never wanted them to stop.

But they did. Declan lifted his head and I looked down my bare body to see him. His eyes were a stormy blue, his lips wet and glistening from my juices. "If this pussy belongs to us, then this virgin ass does, too."

He turned his wrist, left his fingers inside me, but brushed his thumb over that sensitive opening.

I bucked at the feel. My clit was swollen and achy, his fingers still in my pussy. And now this.

"Shh, easy," he said.

I let my head fall back as he continued to play. To circle, to press in.

At first I fought him, my body's instinctive reaction to keep him out. But when he lowered his head again, his tongue working over my clit, I sighed, let everything go lax. It was then that I flowered open and his thumb slipped in.

I heard the lid on the bottle of lube, but I didn't open my eyes. His thumb slipped back and I felt a cool little dribble as he pressed back in, taking the lubricant with it, again and again, adding more and more as he went in deeper.

I was so slippery there that it wasn't painful. Yes, there was a slight burn, a stretching, but it also felt so good. Cole had returned to playing with my breasts and I now appreciated the perks of two mouths and four hands. The things they could do...

"Oh god...fuck," I moaned, unable to hold back. I could keep nothing from them, especially my pleasure when they were so intent, touching me, licking me, working me to the brink, then over.

I screamed, cried out their names, tangled my fingers in their hair.

I lost track of how long it went on. If they were trying to show me how much I was adored...well, mission accomplished. As the orgasm faded, I wasn't sure if any woman had ever been so lavishly sucked and licked and fondled and fingered. They kept going even after I came, my pussy throbbing under Declan's mouth, my ass clenching around his thumb, wanting more, wanting deeper. After I came the second time, I finally called a halt. Well, I didn't ask them to stop, exactly...

"Fuck me," I begged. "I need to be fucked. By both of you. Please."

Those were the magic words.

I was a boneless mass of jelly but when Declan ordered me on all fours I managed to turn over with a little help from my men. Cole settled back on the bed, head on the pillows, Declan came around behind me.

"Do you trust us, darlin'?" Cole asked, his hand lifting to my cheek to stroke it. My breasts hung down, heavy and achy, the tips hard and a little sore from his ardent attentions.

With one playful smack on my ass, I startled, felt my breasts sway.

"Answer him, Hannah," Declan said. He leaned over me and I felt the hot length of his chest press against my back. "Do you trust us?"

"Yes," I replied quickly. There was no reason to delay. I did. I trusted them. Completely. With all of me.

"You want to take us both?" he asked, his lips brushing over my shoulder. A shiver slid down my spine. "I'll be in your ass and Cole deep in your pussy."

"Yes," I breathed.

Cole grinned and crooked his finger and I lifted my knee up and over his hips so I was straddling him. Gripping his cock in my hand, I stroked him once, then again before rising up and aligning that flared tip to my entrance.

He gripped my wrist. "Condom, darlin'." He bit those words out through clenched teeth, knowing he was as eager as I.

I shook my head, bit my lip, released my hold on his cock, which had me lowering onto him, one delicious, big inch at a time. "I'm on the pill."

Cole groaned. "Fuck, Hannah. I've never—"

His words were cut off when I lifted up, then dropped down on him, taking him all the way.

"—gone bare before."

He felt good without any latex separating us. It was all Cole, all sensation.

"I haven't either, but if this is the real deal, then I want nothing between us."

"Christ, that's hot," Declan said, his hand sliding down my back.

"Come here. Give me a kiss." Cole hooked my neck and pulled me down. His mouth was soft, sweet and gentle, completely at odds to what we'd been doing. I felt the love in this, the way his hips lifted and lowered, gently, as if enjoying every moment of us being bare.

I heard the squirt of the lube, the sound of Declan's hand sliding up and down his cock. His coated fingers slipped through my crack and over the hole he was going to soon enter. I was ready for him, he'd made sure of it.

"Me too, sweetheart. Nothing between us," Declan told me as I felt the broad head of his cock pressing against me.

Angled down as I was, he was in perfect alignment to fuck me, so they could both fuck me. Together.

Cole let me up, but held the back of my neck gently. I saw the dark desire in his gaze. "Easy, let Dec in."

I gave him a slight nod and I just stared into his eyes as Declan took hold of my hip, began to press more and more.

"Push back, Hannah. Good. Again. Yes, breathe. I'm almost—"

I groaned when Declan stretched me open and then popped past the resisting ring of muscle.

"Oh my god," I breathed. There was a burn, but not too bad. They'd prepared me well, but I had no idea it would be like this. I was so full, the feelings so intense. No, it was more than intense, it made tears come to my eyes. I felt vulnerable and powerful all at the same time. I'd never been this open, this exposed to anyone before. This had to be the most intimate thing, ever. Yet I felt powerful. I was the one connecting us. I was the one who made us, not a couple, but perhaps the start of a family. I was the center. The heart of it.

"Easy," Cole said again. "Good girl. Just take a minute. Shh."

I wiggled my hips, relaxed my hands on the sheets, arched my back, took the time to adjust. I breathed deeply, willed the silly tears away.

I licked my lips, felt Cole's chest rise and fall, felt his big hands on my hips. Declan caressed a hand down my spine, cupped my bottom. The scent of sex swirled around us, musky and heady. This wasn't a little rutting in the dark. Hell, it wasn't even a quickie on the kitchen table. This was all out fucking. Hot and wet, noisy and sweaty. And I loved it.

I wiggled some more, pushed back and Declan slid in a touch deeper. Cole glanced over my shoulder.

"Ready for more?" Declan asked.

I nodded, my long hair sliding over my bare back.

"Say it, sweetheart. Say you want your men to fuck you together." Declan's words were so carnal, so dark, I shivered.

"I want you...I want you to fuck me together," I whispered, as if I needed to be quiet before the storm.

Cole lifted me up so he slipped from me until only the broad head clung to my swollen folds as Declan slid in more and more. As he pulled back, he applied more lube, easing his way in deep.

I pressed against Cole's chest with my hands, arching my back, rocking my hips as much as I could, my clit rubbing against Cole. It was too much. They were too much. God, *we* were too much.

"I'm...I'm going to come," I gasped. My eyes were closed and I felt sweat bloom across my skin. Cole's body was so hot beneath my palms. Declan's breathing soughed in my ear as I felt his hips press against my bottom.

"I'm in. Fuck, Hannah, you're perfect."

Yes, he was in all the way. So deep, stretching me so open.

He pulled back slowly as Cole plunged deep.

"I'm...it's too much!"

"Come," Cole said, picking up his pace. While I sensed Declan was holding back, he took me in full strokes now, the still tight entry clinging and squeezing his entire length as he moved.

I did come. Perhaps it was because Cole commanded it, but I knew it was just too much. I'd been holding back in life, with my relationship with them and I'd missed out on the pleasure to be had.

And now, I gave myself over to it. I didn't keep anything from my men. I writhed on Cole's lap as I came, my inner walls milking their cocks, wanting them deeper and deeper still.

Declan placed a hand on my shoulder as he

crammed me full, shouted out when he came. He held me in place as he did so, but slowly loosened his grip, let his hand fall away. He carefully slipped from me and I felt his seed follow. Moving to the side, he allowed Cole to grip my hips and flip me onto my back. He pounded into me then, not holding anything back. "God, Hannah. Yes. I love this with you. I love you."

His wild rhythm had me coming again, although I doubted I ever stopped the first time. I brought my knees up, clenched his hips, but he took my ankles and raised them to his shoulders, going even deeper.

He thrust once, twice, then came. I went with him. No limits. No restraints.

I collapsed on his chest, our sweaty bodies clinging, his cock softening within me.

I felt Declan slide in beside me. Cole turned, placed me between them.

"You're ours," Cole said, repeating the possessive words. Yes, they were possessive and now, I felt they even might have been obsessive. Nothing like Brad. They'd been perfect. Perfect for me.

Brad had ruined my life, forced me to flee everything I knew. Yet because of it, I'd found where I belonged. Good from bad. Light from dark.

I reached out and grabbed Declan's bare thigh, put my other hand on Cole's chest.

They'd claimed me, branded me as theirs...and I wouldn't have had it any other way.

"You're mine," I vowed.

I'd have the rest of my life to try, but I knew I'd never get enough of them.

WANT MORE?

———

Read an excerpt of Take Me Fast, book 3 in the Bridgewater County Series!

———

TAKE ME FAST - EXCERPT

VY

Seven years ago

Even through the sleeping bag, the bed of Cooper's rusty old truck was hard beneath my back, but I didn't care. Not when I finally had what I wanted. *Who* I wanted —times two.

Rory was on top of me, his lean yet solid weight settling between my thighs so I could the feel thick outline of his hard cock. My skirt had slid up so my wet panties were pressed against his jeans.

My head was cradled on Cooper's arm and his breath whispered across my cheek as his free hand slipped inside my cotton button-down blouse. Deft fingers found my furled nipple through my lacy bra. I must have moaned because Rory stilled above me, his hips stopped grinding against me and he pulled away from the hot, wet, messy kiss that had started this whole business.

For a second, I thought maybe he was stopping because someone had heard my sound. But, no. We were parked out in the middle of Baker's field, far from town. The night was inky black, only the rising moon offering us light. There was no one around for miles, just the sound of a lone coyote in the distance a reminder of where we were.

It was Cooper who broke the silence, his deep voice gentle by my ear. "Are you sure, Ivy? We've just wanted you for so long. Too long. We don't have to do this if you don't want."

I bit back a groan of frustration, arched my back into his palm. My pussy was aching, throbbing, begging to be fucked. But I wasn't just horny for anyone—I wanted these boys. Both of them. I had for ages.

Cooper and Rory.

We'd grown up together, so I'd known them since forever, but our timing had never been right. By the time they took notice of me, I'd given up hope of them and had a boyfriend. Tom was nice and all, and I'd hoped that he might make me change my mind about Cooper and Rory. I'd watched from a distance as they grew up, filled out...became men. But it wasn't until graduation that I finally called it quits with Tom. I told him it was because I was leaving Bridgewater, off to college in Seattle. That was partly the reason, but I also ended it with him because one thing had become abundantly clear—Tom had never turned me on the way Rory and Cooper did with just a smoldering look across a crowded party or with an easy conversation at one of the high school bonfires. I'd fooled myself long enough. I hadn't had sex with him because I hadn't been ready. I might have been if Tom had been for me. But he wasn't.

I wanted Cooper and Rory and no one else would do. I felt things for them, things I hadn't even understood. At least until now.

My parents had left me with my grandmother when I was a baby and Grandma's idea of the sex talk was to show me some pictures of insects and flowers. None of those pictures prepared me for the firestorm that erupted inside me whenever Cooper and Rory were near. Some sort of electric current between us made my skin hot, my panties wet, and my stomach do flip flops.

I'd thought I'd known what attraction was, but I'd been clueless. Now, thanks to Rory and Cooper, I'd finally gotten a taste of what it meant to be desired and to be wanted, but our timing sucked yet again. If I'd just known they'd been interested sooner. If they'd told me. *If*...enough ifs. Summer was almost over, and once it ended, we'd all be going our separate ways.

Cooper and Rory were still frozen beside and above me, their hands frustratingly still as they waited for my answer. I'd heard some guys just took what they wanted, but not these two. The look of concern was sweet but I couldn't figure out why they'd stopped. This was what I'd wanted for so long—*they* were what I'd wanted—and now it was so close I could taste it, *feel* it. I shifted, trying to get closer to them.

"I'm sure," I breathed, wiggling my hips and making Rory hiss out a breath. I reached up, stroked his dark locks back, although they just fell over his forehead again. "I want my first time to be with you. With both of you."

To most, it would be crazy to be eighteen and want my first time to be with two guys. But this was Bridgewater. Two guys were the norm.

"We weren't thinking it would go this far," Rory said, stroking a thumb over my cheek. Besides having my blouse open a few buttons, we were all still fully dressed. "That you'd want to, at least tonight. Shit, I didn't, um, we don't have any condoms."

"It's okay," I whispered, my cheeks growing hot under their watchful stares, and I hoped they couldn't see it in the moonlight. "I'm on the Pill." I didn't know why I was embarrassed. I wasn't the only girl in our school having sex, or in my case, going to. I'd gone to Dr. Murphy the day I'd turned eighteen. I'd already broken up with Tom, but I'd told myself I wanted to be ready when I got to college.

As I stared up at Rory's heavy-lidded gaze and heard Cooper's labored breathing beside me, I couldn't lie to myself any longer. I'd gone on the Pill because I'd hoped against hope that this would happen. I'd been dreaming about being fucked by these boys for months and now they were acting like they were too gentlemanly to give me what I needed. I loved that about them, but screw it.

Arching my hips up, I pressed my pussy against Rory's erection again. "I know what I'm doing. I want this."

I watched Rory's jaw clench, but he didn't move. He seemed to be waiting for Cooper's verdict.

I turned my head to look at Cooper, the fair-haired one—the sweet and gentle one. Not that Rory wasn't sweet...but he sure as hell wasn't gentle. I knew when they took me, they'd do it just like their personalities; Rory with wild abandon, Cooper with patience and deliberation.

Cooper tucked my hair behind my ear with the hand that had just been fondling my breasts. His pale gaze met mine, held. "God knows we want you so fucking bad, sweets. We always have. But we're going to be leaving soon..."

A whole new kind of ache swept over me. Sadness. Regret. Something close to nostalgia, even though that didn't make any sense at all. We all knew that this would be the one and only chance we had since I was leaving for college in a couple days and these boys had enlisted in the army. We were in a little bubble in the back of the pickup. Alone. Together. Safe.

This was it. Our one chance.

I forced a smile for Cooper's sake. "I know." I drew in a deep breath. "All the more reason for us to have this one night, don't you think?"

Cooper grinned and leaned in to give me a long, lingering kiss as Rory growled above me. He started grinding against me again and I spread my legs wider, giving him total access.

My words worked. All hesitation was gone and both boys sprang into action, fumbling with the remainder of the buttons on my shirt and the zipper of my skirt. Rory gave up on the skirt and tugged my panties off in one move. They raced to take off their own clothes and soon I was staring up at two very naked, very *hot* young men.

My mouth gaped when I caught sight of their cocks standing at attention as they hovered over me. Holy shit, they were big and they were ready. I'd seen pictures of them in magazines and online, but they weren't anything like this. Thick and long, hard too, both pointed right at me.

After that it was something of a blur. We were all hands and mouths as we greedily groped and kissed and licked and sucked.

Cooper took me first, settling between my parted thighs and nudging at my eager entrance. He swallowed the cry of pain as he carefully took my virginity. As he did so, Rory whispered in my ear telling me how beautiful I was, how perfect we were together, how he couldn't wait to have me. He reached between Cooper and I, found my clit with his thumb as Cooper continued to slowly move. To slide deep then pull almost all the way out. The combination was too much. I clawed at his back, pulling him deeper, wanting more. Faster. Wanting it all. I threw my head back and screamed up at the stars. After that, I lost track of how many times they made me come, how many times they took turns fucking me. Until the three of us were lost in each other, until there was nothing between us.

GET A FREE BOOK!

ABOUT THE AUTHOR

Vanessa Vale is the *USA Today* Bestselling author of over 40 books, sexy romance novels, including her popular Bridgewater historical romance series and hot contemporary romances featuring unapologetic bad boys who don't just fall in love, they fall hard. When she's not writing, Vanessa savors the insanity of raising two boys, is figuring out how many meals she can make with a pressure cooker, and teaches a pretty mean karate class. While she's not as skilled at social media as her kids, she loves to interact with readers.

BookBub

www.vanessavaleauthor.com

ALSO BY VANESSA VALE

Bridgewater County Series

Ride Me Dirty

Claim Me Hard

Take Me Fast

Hold Me Close

Make Me Yours

Kiss Me Crazy

Mail Order Bride of Slate Springs Series

A Wanton Woman

A Wild Woman

A Wicked Woman

Bridgewater Ménage Series

Their Runaway Bride

Their Kidnapped Bride

Their Wayward Bride

Their Captivated Bride

Their Treasured Bride

Their Christmas Bride